NOT YOUR ALL-AMERICAN GIRL

NOT YOUR ALL-AMERICAN GIRL

MADELYN ROSENBERG &
WENDY WAN-LONG SHANG

Scholastic Inc.

To the grandmothers who rock our world

—MRR & WWS

CHAPTER 1

ROYAL WE

MY FIFTH-GRADE TEACHER ONCE
said that Tara and I were the Royal We. "We didn't like today's lunch," I told her after we had been served sandwiches with meat that had weird jellied circles. It was like someone had tried to turn bologna into a stained-glass window.

"May we please use the bathroom?"

"When do we get to take Lola home for the weekend?" (Lola was the class guinea pig.)

"It's always the Royal We with you two, isn't it?" said Mrs. Mortson.

I hadn't heard the term *royal we* before, but it made sense, because I always felt a bit grander when Tara was around. Being with Tara was like being in a patch of sunshine. She was the one teachers loved and the one who always got picked early for teams in PE. She was the one who got a blue ribbon at the science fair. She was the one someone was always saving a seat for in the cafeteria. But she sat with me. And I was the one she gave the other half of the best friends necklace to.

I have contributed to our mutual royalty exactly once, when we tried out for the school Christmas concert as a duet in fourth grade. I felt a little weird, trying out for a Christmas concert as someone who does not celebrate Christmas. We sang "Winter Wonderland," which does not specifically mention Christmas, so that no one in my family got upset. Tara said we got it because of me. But in everything else, the spotlight was on Tara.

I thought of it this way: In your typical Pac-Man lunch box, Tara was the PB&J, and I was the apple. You needed both to have a complete meal, even if one was the star. Tara was the star of our friendship.

I found out later that the Royal We was something that kings and queens used instead of "I." Queen Victoria supposedly said, "We are not amused," after someone told a scandalous story in her presence. Tara and I still say this whenever my brother tells a so-called joke or when my father asks me to take out the garbage. I can do the British accent with just the right amount of snobbiness.

Most of the time, everything's better with the Royal We.

But being the Royal We hasn't always worked out. For instance, the Royal We had to stay inside during recess three times in Mrs. Mortson's class for talking too much.

In October, the Royal We did not win WKRZ concert tickets to see The Police. And only half of the Royal We got designer jeans, because the other half has unreasonable parents who do not see the value of "having someone else's name embroidered on your hiney." On top of that, this year, in sixth grade, the Royal We faced our biggest battle yet: The only class we had together was science. Not even lunch. After nearly six months in the sixth grade, no one at Dwight D. Eisenhower Junior High knew the Royal We existed.

"I have the solution," Tara said. One of the good things about being the Royal We, even if we were invisible, was that Tara could start with a sentence like this, and I'd know if she was talking about the solution to the designer jeans problem (she wasn't) or the solution to us not spending enough time together (she was).

"Tell," I said.

"The musical!" she said.

"Are there duets?"

"We'll probably be in the ensemble, being sixth graders, but it would still be awesome," said Tara. "Because we would be together." Then she added, "Unless you get the lead."

"Like that's going to happen."

"It totally could!" That was one thing I loved about Tara: She saw possibilities for me even when I couldn't.

The day of tryouts, Tara and I both wore purple socks, because those were our lucky socks. We had both picked out our songs and practiced. I had wanted my mom to help me prepare, because she had a good ear, but she was out of town. I was on my own, which mostly meant singing while I was in the shower or walking to school.

"I'm going to be late," Tara said when we met by my locker at the end of the day. "You have to go without me."

Tara got kind of quiet and drew a line on the floor with the toe of her sneaker. For a minute, I thought something was wrong. Then she said, "I made the finals of the oratory contest. I have to meet with Mrs. Loft."

The oratory contest was a really big tradition. I suppose that's why they called it "oratory" instead of "speech," because it went back so many years. We all had to give speeches in our English classes, and the top students from each class competed against one another. The teachers picked six finalists in each grade, who competed for the school championship, and the winner of that went on to compete against other kids in the county.

I'd written my speech on the world's most disastrous Thanksgiving, when my brother nearly choked to death on a piece of turkey. It got some laughs, because he survived, and my English teacher said that she was going to show it to our health teacher, who then talked about the importance of chewing before swallowing. But it was not the kind of speech that teachers liked. They wanted something that talked about how wonderful the world could be if everybody got along.

I gave Tara a hug. "Congratulations! It's an excellency!" That was our word for when something really fantastic happened. I sang it out, the way you'd sing in an opera. "You . . . shall . . . be . . . the . . . best!!!" I got super high at the last part and held the note. Some teachers stopped and applauded.

"It's just a speech," said Tara.

I had heard her speech when she was practicing before school. We didn't have to memorize our speeches, but Tara had memorized every word of hers, and when she talked, she walked around and used a lot of hand gestures. Her speech was called "Getting the Best from Yourself and Others."

"Your speech is catnip for teachers," I said, even though we didn't have a cat. "But talk fast so you don't miss tryouts."

"Don't worry," she said. "I'll be there."

Our school musical was going to be a production called *Shake It Up*, which was actually written by our drama teacher. It was set in 1958, the year that Hula-Hoops became popular in the United States. The main character, all-American girl Brenda Sue Parker, wants everyone to love Hula-Hoops because her dad owns the toy store in Pleasant Valley, a charming all-American town. But some of the townspeople think Hula-Hoops are evil because you have to shake your hips to keep them going. Brenda Sue invites world-famous hip shaker Elvis Presley to Pleasant Valley to teach the townspeople a valuable lesson about innovation and self-expression, but it is really Brenda Sue's love of Hula-Hooping that wins everyone over.

I got the inside information from Hector, who saw *Shake It Up* when the community theater performed it two years ago. Even if he hadn't seen it, Hector would have talked about it. He'll go with any conversational topic you give him. I've known Hector for a long time because he's my brother's best friend. He's also possibly the only student at Eisenhower Junior High who makes my brother, David, seem normal in comparison. Hector never tried to be cool; when he was excited about something, you knew it.

"Elvis had a song called 'Rock-A-Hula Baby,'" said Hector.

"Elvis died on a toilet," I said. I knew from experience that you have to volley back something to the trivia nerds, or they'll try to take over the whole conversation, and then you're trapped. I knew a lot about Elvis because I had the same birthday as his daughter, Lisa Marie.

"It's a terrible way to go. Get it? *Go.*" Hector laughed so hard he made a reverse-snorting sound and people turned around to look at him.

"Speaking of going," I said. "Tryouts are in ten minutes." I was trying to stay calm, but the electric, buzzy feeling in my head was getting stronger.

"You'll be great!" shouted Hector. "Good luck!" Anyone who hadn't turned around for Hector's reverse-snorting was now turning around to see who he was shouting at.

I made a tiny wave, which I hoped Hector would take as both a goodbye gesture and a please-stop-being-embarrassing motion. Instead, he followed me into the auditorium. I wished Tara had been with me instead.

CHAPTER 2

SILENCE, THESPIANS

MRS. TYNDALL, THE DIRECTOR, WAS tall and had good posture, so when she stood on the stage and we were in the seats, she seemed gigantic. Also, she had a cane. No one had ever seen her use it on a student, but there were rumors.

"This show requires discipline," Mrs. Tyndall said. She thumped the cane like a scepter. "Discipline and commitment. If you are not committed to the full vision of this production, you are welcome to leave now."

"How can we know what the full vision is if she hasn't told us?" asked a kid sitting behind me. I wondered the same thing.

"Silence, thespians!" said Mrs. Tyndall. I had imagined a theater teacher would wear flowy clothes and move her hands a lot. But she sounded more like Mr. Surface, the vice principal, whose last known smile was in 1974. "Now. Those of you who are trying out for smaller parts will go first. Those of you trying for leads will go last. Please be sure to mark the square on your form indicating whether or not you are willing to take an ensemble part. When we call your name, you will hand your form to Miss Ellison." She used her cane to point at a student sitting in a chair to the side of the stage. "Then you will proceed to the center to begin your audition. There are a lot of you, and we need to get through everyone this afternoon. I will post callbacks on the door tomorrow morning."

The form asked for my Hula-Hoop skill level—*1* for beginner, *2* for intermediate, or *3* for advanced. I picked *2*. The form also asked for my performing experience, which wasn't much, even though I loved to sing. Under recitals, I wrote, *Performed at Etz Hayim Synagogue for an audience of 103*, which was the number of people who had come to my brother's bar mitzvah. I debated whether or not to include my role as celery for a play about the food groups in second grade. In the end, I left that one off.

"I remember that," said Hector, looking over my shoulder. He was talking about the bar mitzvah, not the celery.

"Duh. It wasn't that long ago," I said.

"No, I mean, I remember you were good. Like, professional good."

I stopped writing to look at Hector and see if he was

teasing me. Other people had said nice things about my singing, but I figured that they felt obligated. Hector didn't have to say anything.

"Thanks," I said, turning my head away so he couldn't see me blush.

———————————————

Duncan Stowell, whose sister had been in the musicals before, said if you didn't get a lead, you could still end up with a minor part or in the ensemble as long as you checked the little square. So you may as well try for the big parts. Nearly everybody did. Duncan was trying out for Mayor McArdle, although I wasn't sure he looked old enough. He was skinny, with curly hair and braces. If you saw him walking down the street, you would think, "I'll bet that kid is twelve." Some of the eighth graders could pass for real-life mayors.

"Where's Tara?" Duncan asked. "Isn't she trying out?"

"If she gets here in time," I said. "She's supposed to come after she wins her next award."

I adjusted the buttons on my jean jacket. Sometimes people called me The Button Girl because buttons—the kind with funny sayings on them—are my trademark. It is important to have a trademark when you have a friend like Tara so that you don't seem like a side dish all the time.

In honor of today's audition, I had put on an ALL THE WORLD'S A STAGE button and one with a rainbow ending in a star.

Duncan nodded as Mrs. Tyndall started calling the boys to the stage.

Hector tried out singing "Hound Dog," which is an Elvis song. He was surprisingly good. I was having a hard time deciding who was better, him or Ricky Almond, who was basically the eighth-grade equivalent of Tara at school. Duncan tried out with a different Elvis song, "Heartbreak Hotel." He wasn't as good as Hector, but he wasn't bad.

When the boys were done, a few of them stuck around to watch the girls. I saw Tara sneak in, too. She quietly closed the door to the auditorium so it wouldn't slam. When it was my turn, she moved to a front-side seat, so I would be able to see her from the stage.

"Lauren Horowitz."

I walked toward the stage with this weird trembly feeling, like something really great or really terrible was about to happen.

"You," Mrs. Tyndall said. "You're Brenda Sue!"

For a second, I thought she was talking to me. For that same second, I saw myself in the spotlight, holding a microphone while people applauded wildly.

But Mrs. Tyndall was pointing behind me.

"My name's Tara," Tara said, looking confused.

Mrs. Tyndall laughed in a theatrical way. "I meant Brenda Sue Parker," she said. "The quintessential all-American girl of the 1950s."

I knew what Mrs. Tyndall meant. Tara had reddish-brown

hair and blue eyes, and her skin was milky and clear. She had freckles sprinkled across her nose. "A dusting" was what they called it in the magazines. Tara twisted her face in an I-doubt-it kind of way. Her mother was big on what it meant to be female in the 1980s, so maybe she thought this was a step backward. "It's Lauren's turn," she said.

Mrs. Tyndall looked at me with the same expression my mom uses when she inspects the fruit at the grocery store. "Well. Lauren, do you have your music?"

Mrs. Tyndall said we could sing any song we wanted. She cut everyone off after two minutes. Some people picked songs from the show, and some people picked "Happy Birthday" or "The Star-Spangled Banner" because those songs show how well you can stay on key, even if "Happy Birthday" is much shorter than two minutes. Instead I picked "Girls Just Want to Have Fun," because Brenda Sue sounded like a girl who wanted to have fun. It spoke to my character's motivation.

I handed my music to the accompanist. On the radio, the song starts with a snappy synthesizer, drums, and electric guitar. I didn't have any of those things, so my song felt a little bare as the accompanist played the first few bars. But once I hit that first high note, I knew I was good. In the original song, Cyndi Lauper's voice sounds like a New Yorker's, kind of nasally and a little harsh, but fun at the same time. I got this jumpy feeling as I looked out at the audience. They were all watching me, smiling and bobbing their heads. I skipped around the stage, the way Cyndi Lauper does in the music video, as much as I could with the microphone on a cord. I got applause for that move.

Tara gave me a thumbs-up. Around the two-minute mark, I held out the microphone for the chorus and everyone sang along. Mrs. Tyndall let me go over the two minutes. It was amazing. A thousand excellencies smooshed together.

"Thank you, Lauren," Mrs. Tyndall said. I hopped off the stage and went to sit by Tara.

"You owned that stage!" Tara said.

A girl I knew from Home Ec came over. "I thought I was tired of hearing Cyndi Lauper on the radio," she whispered. "But you made me like the song again."

"Thanks," I whispered back.

We watched a few more auditions while we were waiting for Tara's turn. Suddenly I felt more confident. No one was getting the reaction that I got.

"Settle down, everyone," said Mrs. Tyndall, after an eighth grader sang a song by Madonna. She checked her list. "Tara Buchanan."

Tara smiled at me.

"Go for it," I whispered.

"There's no way I'll be as good as you," she said.

"Maybe we'll both get leads." I gave her a thumbs-up.

Tara got onstage and handed her music to the pianist. I knew what she was going to sing—"The Candy Man." We had rented the movie *Willy Wonka & the Chocolate Factory* from the video store and sang along for practice.

She started too high, but then she got the song into the right range. She stayed in one spot and did not move around, although she did use some hand gestures, like in oratory. Everyone clapped when she finished; I clapped the loudest.

Tara came offstage and sank into her seat—as much as a person could sink into auditorium seats that were made of wood. I liked to think about the people whose initials were carved into them. Were T. A. and C. B. married now? Did Mr. Shulter still suck eggs?

"You were definitely better," Tara said. "I mean, with the oratory contest, I'm not sure I could even do it if I got a part."

"You'll get a part," I said.

Secretly I was imagining myself as Brenda Sue, and Tara in the ensemble. Normally Tara was the one who shined a little brighter. On swim team, we both swam in the B meets, but only Tara swam in the A meets. Last year, when we worked on our history projects, only Tara got a "Superb!" I got a "Nice work, Lauren" without an exclamation point.

In the play, we would be the Royal We again. Only this time, I would be the peanut butter and jelly sandwich.

CHAPTER 3

STAR SEARCH

WHEN I GOT HOME FROM SCHOOL, my grandmothers were attempting to watch *Star Search* on the VCR. *Star Search* is a talent show where the challengers try to beat the champions in categories like singing, dancing, and comedy. Wai Po, my Chinese grandmother, lives with us, and Safta, my Jewish grandmother, lives around the corner. It's convenient for arguing and watching *Star Search*. It's the only thing they have in common besides me; my brother, David; and Burt Bacharach, the man who wrote "Raindrops Keep Fallin' on My Head."

They've been fighting over me pretty much since I was a baby, when Safta wanted to put me in lacy pink or white dresses, and Wai Po said white was for mourning and that I should wear red, a happy, lucky color. Sometimes I feel like a toy being pulled between them, each grandmother hoping

I'll be more Jewish or more Chinese. But right then, if you asked me what I was, I would say: a singer.

Wai Po stabbed at every button on the VCR. "David said he recorded it for me," she said. Making a recording on the VCR was always dicey because you weren't sure you'd done it right until after the show you wanted was over. The TV screen remained stubbornly dark.

"Did you remember to change the input?" Safta prided herself on keeping up with technology.

"Of course! I changed all the inputs."

"Did you change the TV channel to three?"

"It's on three."

"I could just tell you who won," Safta said.

"I don't want to know. I want to watch," said Wai Po.

Watching *Star Search* is a ritual in my house on Sunday nights. Only this week, Wai Po missed it for mahjong. David, I suspected, watched for the spokesmodels, but he paid attention to the other categories, too. We usually agreed with each other on who should win, but we didn't always agree with the judges.

Safta and I had a ritual at the end of the show. "Those teen singers were good," she would say when Ed McMahon brought out the winners and shook their hands while everyone was dancing. "But they're no Lauren Horowitz." And then I would say, "Safta," and roll my eyes, like it was the silliest thing she could say. But here's what nobody knew, not even Tara: I spent large amounts of time wondering if I could sing on *Star Search*. If I got a part in the play, maybe it would be a sign.

"I like that Sam Harris," said Wai Po, pushing the VCR button one last time. "I hope he moves on to next week."

"Well," Safta said. "It is your lucky day."

"I told you not to tell me," Wai Po said.

"All I said was that it's your lucky day."

Wai Po changed the inputs again. "So now we don't need to watch." In a way, she seemed relieved.

"How was school?" asked Safta. Since my mom, who was a paralegal, was away working on a trial for most of the week, my grandmothers were trying to fill in for her. The big things they did were making sure we ate something besides breakfast cereal and asking about school.

I couldn't hold it in anymore. "My audition went great! I'm definitely going to get a good part. I think."

"Keinehora!" said Safta. "Spit!" She believed that saying something good will happen brings bad luck. Spitting is supposed to cancel it out, although there is no scientific evidence to support this. I pretended to spit. *Pooh, pooh, pooh.*

"Of course you will get a good part. You have a beautiful voice," said Wai Po. But she didn't sound happy about it.

"What are you doing?" said Safta. "Now you spit."

"Fine." Wai Po leaned over and spit for real into a wastebasket. "This is silly."

"Says the woman who told me not to sweep the floor last month."

"You want to sweep away your fortune? Next Chinese New Year you sweep, but at your own house."

"We always knew you were going to be a star," Safta said to me. "The bar mitzvah confirmed it." For some reason, Safta didn't feel like she had to spit when she said this.

"A doctor is the star of the OR," Wai Po said. "An accountant is the star of tax season. A lawyer is the star of the courtroom."

"So she'll be a Broadway star who finds a cure for cancer," said Safta. "She can be anything she wants." This was something my mother always said, too.

She seemed to have forgotten that blood and diseases were not my favorite subject.

"I'm going upstairs to do my homework," I told them. Then I sang, "Homework! It's time to do my homework! I'd rather sing than do my homework! But I don't have a choice!"

I bowed and ran upstairs. My main homework was studying for a math quiz on negative numbers. Before I started, I got out my button maker from under the bed. It was a Hanukkah gift from my parents, because I wore so many buttons and they thought it would be fun—and cheaper—if I made my own. A button maker wasn't the same as designer jeans, which was what I'd originally wanted. These were jeans made by famous fashion designers, like Gloria Vanderbilt and Calvin Klein. Their names were signed in thread on the back pocket, the way artists signed their paintings. Dad said maybe I could write Gloria Vanderbilt's name on a button and pin that to my back pocket. For a nurse, he wasn't thinking through the dangers very well.

I decided to make a button that would commemorate the play tryouts. It couldn't be obvious. It couldn't say "No. 1 Hula-Hooper" or "A star is born!" Since I had a math quiz, I settled on

I thought I might even show it to my math teacher, Mrs. Fink, who had a good sense of humor for someone who inflicted mathematical torture on students. I guess anyone named Fink would have to have a good sense of humor, for self-preservation.

On the way to school the next day, I saw tons of things that reminded me of hoops. A Circle Tour bus. A Buick with its round logo. The wheels on a bicycle. Were there always so many round things on my way to school, or was it a sign about my future?

When I got to school, I heard someone say, "There's the girl I was telling you about," and wondered if they meant me. Ann Hooper, who was a friend of a friend and actually had the word *hoop* in her name, gave me a thumbs-up.

Normally I would have felt nervous, waiting for a teacher to post something like callbacks. This time, I was excited. Everything in my life was going to start as soon as Mrs. Tyndall taped those papers outside her door, right before the first lunch shift.

Tara passed me a note during science: *YOU ARE GOING TO BE A ★!* We had to pass notes because Mr. Kirby was like our elementary school teachers who said we talked too much when we sat together. As soon as the bell rang, Tara and I ran-walked toward Mrs. Tyndall's classroom, which was at the other end of the school. I got to go to lunch, but Tara would have to go to class as soon as we saw the list.

"Everyone is talking about your audition," Tara said between breaths.

"I hope we both get parts," I said. I figured we could practice in my room. The bed could be a stage.

"I hope, I hope, I hope," she said.

Mrs. Tyndall had made two lists. One said *ENSEMBLE* and one said *CALLBACKS FOR MAJOR ROLES*. My heart beat faster as I searched for the names that made up the Royal We.

CHAPTER 4

NO CALLBACK

ENSEMBLE

Please note: This list is not complete. Others will be joining your ranks after callbacks tomorrow.

LAUREN HOROWITZ

HALLELUJAH SIMMONS

MICHAEL SPIERS

DUNCAN STOWELL

CHERYL VICKERS

I was not the star. I was not even under consideration for being the star. All the air squeezed out of my lungs, leaving them flat and heavy. But that wasn't the worst part.

CALLBACKS FOR MAJOR ROLES
BRENDA SUE PARKER:

TARA BUCHANAN

JENNIFER GALLAGHER

CHAPTER 5

A GIRL FROM PLEASANT VALLEY

"IT'S GOT TO BE A MISTAKE," TARA said.

"It's not—my name is over here." I pointed to the *ENSEMBLE* list. "And your name is over here." I pointed to the *CALLBACKS* list. "Congratulations."

"Maybe Mrs. Tyndall got confused," said Tara. "And left your name off by accident."

"And put it on the ensemble list? Maybe my singing just sucks." I tried to say it like a joke, but even as I said it, my heart tightened up. If Mrs. Tyndall said that, I might die. Anyway, that wasn't what anyone else had said. Not my grandmothers. Not Hector, who was a finalist for Theodore Goreson, the boy who Brenda Sue likes. Not the strangers in the hall. Not my best friend.

"We should ask Mrs. Tyndall about it," Tara said firmly. We. The Royal We.

This was why adults liked Tara—because she knew how to get stuff done. The door to Mrs. Tyndall's office was closed, but we could tell she was in there. Tara knocked before I could back out.

"Hello, girls," said Mrs. Tyndall. "Lauren and Tara, right?"

"That's right," Tara said.

I looked at her and shook my head. *Let's not do this.*

Tara said, "Mrs. Tyndall, we just checked the lists, and we wondered if Lauren was supposed to be on the callback list. She had a really good audition, didn't she?"

"Lauren did have a good audition. That's why she's been cast," said Mrs. Tyndall. She smiled, and I couldn't tell if she was acting. "You also had a good audition."

"Thanks," Tara said. "We just wondered"—Mrs. Tyndall didn't know about the Royal We—"if Lauren was supposed to get a callback for Brenda Sue, too."

I wanted to hug Tara. But Mrs. Tyndall didn't look like she wanted to hug anybody. She sighed and took off her glasses. "You definitely have some musical talent," she said to me. "But I have to consider the audience. You don't want the audience to be taken out of the story for any reason. The audience comes to the theater for ninety minutes of magic. Right?"

We nodded.

"So when we go to the town of Pleasant Valley, Tennessee, we want to see it onstage: an all-American town trying to do what's right for its young people."

Something inside me started to feel like one of those dreams where you begin to fall. And keep falling. "I have a second cousin in Tennessee," I said, though I knew that was not the point.

"Look at Tara," said Mrs. Tyndall. "When people see her, they won't have a hard time imagining she's an all-American girl from Pleasant Valley. It's our job in the theater to make it easy for the audience to imagine they are right there with her."

She made it sound so reasonable.

She said: *Tara looks like she's from Pleasant Valley.*

She meant: *You look like you're from someplace else. Someplace that isn't Pleasant Valley. Someplace that isn't even in the United States.* Why hadn't I sung "The Star-Spangled Banner" for my tryout instead?

"You'll do a great job in the group numbers. You'll help everyone stay on pitch," said Mrs. Tyndall. "Don't forget, every role is important, or it wouldn't be there. Most girls would feel extremely lucky to make the ensemble."

I would have felt extremely lucky to be in the ensemble, too, if Mrs. Tyndall hadn't said what she'd said. And if Tara wasn't poised to be the peanut butter and jelly. Again.

"Won't the audience wonder why there's one Chinese Jewish girl in Pleasant Valley?" I asked, just to show her that I got her point about sticking out. Though there was only one Chinese Jewish girl at Eisenhower Junior High, too.

"You're Jewish?" said Mrs. Tyndall. "Are you sure?"

I wanted to say I wouldn't have spent so much time being bored out of my mind in Hebrew school if I weren't Jewish, but I decided against it. The Chinese part of me was the part she could see, but the Jewish part of me was always there, too.

Mrs. Tyndall made a little sweeping motion with her hand. "Anyway, that's the ensemble. They'll barely notice."

Because I was an apple. A French fry. A green bean and corn and macaroni and cheese. I was the side dish. I didn't have reddish-brown hair or blue eyes. I had black hair and brown eyes like my mom and a dimply smile like my dad. Some girls in my grade liked to put their arms against mine

25

and say how tan I was, even at the end of winter. I had thought that was a good thing. Until now.

"What about Hector Clelland?" I asked. Hector's mom was Cuban, and Hector had her almost-black wavy hair and dark eyes, but his skin was lighter than hers. It was lighter than mine, possibly from spending so much time in the basement playing Atari. I crossed my fingers that I hadn't just messed up his callback.

"Hector?" Mrs. Tyndall wrinkled her forehead. "Well, Hector looks like your all-American boy."

Because he is all-American, I thought. *Like me.*

"I'm just talking about appearances," Mrs. Tyndall said. "Pleasant Valley."

The Royal We walked out of Mrs. Tyndall's office together. I couldn't look at Tara, her blue eyes and freckles. She was also wearing her Gloria Vanderbilt jeans. They fit her perfectly. The one time I'd tried them on, I'd had to roll up the cuffs.

"Are you okay?" she asked.

"Fine," I said. The less I spoke, the smaller the chance that I would start crying.

"I was *so* sure there was a mistake," said Tara. "Really. But I guess I kind of get her point? About the audience?" She stopped. "I bet it's also because we don't have a lot of Chinese kids in our school. Like, there aren't enough kids to look like your family." Brenda Sue had a brother and two parents in the play.

"My dad isn't Chinese," I pointed out.

"Right, but at least one of your parents should be Chinese," she said. In our school, that left my brother, David, who was allergic to acting.

"Why couldn't Brenda Sue be adopted?" I said.

"She could be, I guess. But maybe that didn't happen a lot in the fifties?" She looked as if she was trying to solve a math problem.

I knew that she was trying to make me feel better, so I tried not to feel worse.

"Don't be sad," she said. "We'll be together. We'll have fun. And if I don't get the part, maybe I'll be in the ensemble, too." She said this like there was a chance she wouldn't get it.

"I'm okay," I said. I tried to squeeze my disappointment as far down as it would go and pasted a smile on my face as I went to the cafeteria and Tara went to English. I didn't want to mess up her chances of getting the starring role because I was sad. That's not what a good friend would do, right?

Sneaking into my house when you didn't want to talk to anybody was hard. Even James Bond couldn't have done it. I could usually make it past my dad or my brother okay. Wai Po's dog, Bao Bao, didn't bark when people came into the house; he barked when they were *already* inside. But the women in my house had bionic hearing.

I let out the smallest sigh when I was just outside my bedroom. It was such a relief to be home, to not have to pretend to be okay anymore.

"Was that Lauren?" asked Safta from down in the living room.

"Of course it was Lauren," said Wai Po. "I heard her coming through the door."

"I heard her outside, when she was on the street," said Safta.

"How can you hear her on the street when you do not hear me when I ask you to help fold laundry during *General Hospital*?"

"I have excellent hearing," said Safta. "Especially when it comes to Lauren." She switched to her shouting voice, which wasn't so different from her regular voice. "Lauren?"

I had two choices: I could crawl out the upstairs window and shimmy down the drainpipe like they do in movies. Or I could answer them.

"I'm doing my homework," I called from the stairs. I wished Mom were home. Mom knew when it was a good time to ask questions and when you just needed someone to sit quietly with you. This was not my grandmothers' specialty.

"Good. Homework is important," said Wai Po. "Grades are important."

"She knows," said Safta.

"I did not say she did not know," Wai Po said.

I walked slowly back downstairs with my backpack still on my shoulder. They were going to find out sooner or later.

"So. How did it go?" asked Safta, her voice clearly expecting a certain outcome.

"I'm not one of the stars," I said. "I'm in the ensemble." The *Schoolhouse Rock!* song "I'm Just a Bill" pushed its way into my head with the sad-looking rolled-up piece of paper. *I'm just a side dish, yes, I'm only a side dish.*

"Ensemble?" asked Safta. "Are you sure there isn't a mistake?"

"It's not a mistake," I said. "I checked. Like, really checked with the teacher and everything."

"Maybe it's better this way," said Wai Po. "You can be in the play but still focus on school."

"And you made it into the play!" Safta said. "The ensemble is wonderful. You'll get to sing! Maybe they were saving the big parts for the eighth graders."

"Maybe," I said. And then I blurted out all of the things I'd been holding inside all day. "I didn't even make callbacks. It was mostly eighth graders who got callbacks, but Tara got one. The teacher basically said she was Brenda Sue Parker. The star."

My grandmothers sucked in their breath at the same time. If there had been any bugs in the room, they would have been vacuumed right up.

"What's going on?" said my dad, coming in from the kitchen. Bao Bao chose that moment to start barking. He'd been barking more since Wai Po had put him on a diet.

"Can't you (*yap*) get him (*yap*) some (*yap*) manners (*yap yap*)?" asked Safta. She and Bao Bao had warmed up to each other, but she still thought he needed refining. Wai Po picked up Bao Bao and put him on her lap to get him to shush.

Safta looked over at me to see if I was going to give my dad the latest theatrical bulletin. When I didn't, she said, "Lauren has suffered a disappointment." She made it sound as if I had broken my arm or something.

"The play?" asked my dad.

I nodded.

"You didn't get a part?" my dad said.

"I got one," I said.

"Well, that's great!" He was obviously relieved.

"I'm in the ensemble," I said.

"Fantastic!" He came over and kissed me on the fore-head. "Be sure to tell your mom when she gets home. You'll be the best Hula-Hooper Pleasant Valley has ever seen."

"With the best voice," said Safta.

"And the smartest brain," added Wai Po.

"No one cares how smart you are when you're in the ensemble," I said. "They only care about the stars."

"You're the star in our hearts," said Safta.

I tried to let their words wash over me, like a warm bath. And they were right: It was good that I was in the ensemble. Some people who tried out wouldn't be anything. It didn't make sense, but somehow, I felt like I had let everyone down by not looking more all-American.

CHAPTER 6

DISCOVERING PATSY KLEIN AND WTRY

MY BROTHER, DAVID, LIKES TRIVIA, so this was his attempt to make me feel better when he came into my room: "Did you know Sylvester Stallone got turned down for the role of Han Solo?"

"So?" I said.

"So people get rejected all the time, and they still do great stuff. Sylvester Stallone won an Oscar for *Rocky*."

That was true.

"Technically Stallone wasn't turned down," David continued. "He took himself out of the running. He said that he didn't think someone who looked like him seemed like he belonged in space."

This was one of those times I wished I had stopped David

from going on one of his trivia tangents. Mrs. Tyndall probably thought I didn't look like I belonged in space, either. If she had been casting *Star Wars*, she probably would have made me a stormtrooper so my face would be all covered up by a helmet.

"That's the thing," I said. "I don't look like I belong anywhere." I told him about Tara and the all-American girl.

"You belong," David said.

"Prove it."

I could see the wheels turning in his head. "The category is . . . musicals that Lauren could star in." He paused. "I might need to call Hector. That's really more his specialty."

David and I shared the receiver while he called Hector and explained the situation.

"Lauren not getting a callback is the crime of the century," Hector said. "She had the best audition." That made me feel a tiny bit better.

"Focus on the question," said David. "We need a part where Lauren looks like she belongs."

"Well, *The King and I* takes place in Siam," Hector said. "But, uh, the female lead is white. Siam is the old name for Thailand."

David put his hand over the mouthpiece. "This could take a while," he told me.

"Does it have to be a Broadway play? Could it be a movie?" asked Hector.

"Sure," I said.

"Or a TV show?"

"Sure."

There was a long pause. "The village women in *M*A*S*H*?" said Hector timidly. *M*A*S*H* was a TV show set during the Korean War.

"They don't *sing*," I said.

"Let me ask my grandmother," said Hector. He put down the phone and came back a few minutes later. "Rodgers and Hammerstein. *South Pacific*. There's a character named Bloody Mary who is Polynesian. She sings."

"Bloody Mary?" I asked. "What kind of name is that?"

"I don't know. I haven't seen it," Hector said.

David and Hector then veered off into a conversation about whether Bruce Lee, the martial arts star, ever did any singing. Then David hung up.

"So, are you okay now?" he asked.

I tried to feel grateful. But one show featuring some-one named Bloody Mary did not feel like enough. One just proved how few there were. I shrugged.

"Do you mind if I turn on the game?" asked David, who clearly thought he had carried out his brotherly duties. "Scott and I bet tomorrow's snack cake on it."

"Sure."

The closest baseball team to us was the Baltimore Orioles, and on a clear night, you could pick up the games on the radio. But as David hunted around for the station on the radio, instead of the twang of a baseball game announcer, this pure, haunting voice started singing about being lonely and blue.

"Stop," I said.

"That's country music," said David. "No one listens to country music, at least not in this house."

"Why not?"

David gave me a long stare. "It's for people who live in the country and ride horses and drive trucks," he said. "Not exactly our family." He meant because we were Jewish, because we were Chinese. Because we were both. He reached for the dial again.

"Change the station, and I'll change you," I threatened.

"Fine," he said. "But I'm taking your Walkman." He put the headphones on and went out of the room. I closed the door and listened to the rest of the song.

The singer's voice was a mixture of mountains and longing. I felt her loneliness, but I felt connected to her, too. For the first time all day, it seemed like someone understood me.

I checked the dial. It was around 102. The DJ came on and said I was listening to WTRY, which I had always skipped over in favor of the Top 40 stations. But that voice changed things. The DJ didn't announce the singer's name. I had to know who she was.

I went downstairs and grabbed the phone book, just as Mom walked through the front door. She put down a small suitcase.

"I hope you're not calling someone this late," she said, just like that. She'd been gone for almost a week, and she didn't skip a beat in the Mom department. "Tara?"

"No," I said. *It's easier to be a good friend if I don't talk to her,* I thought, but I didn't want to unload on Mom right as she walked in. That usually made her grumpy. I gave her a hug to welcome her home. "How was the trial?"

"The judge really had it in for one of our attorneys," she said. "But I think we put on a good case."

"Did you win?"

"We don't get to find out right away." She pushed back her hair. Her eyes looked more tired than usual. "How was the tryout?"

"I got a part, but . . ." Just then Dad walked in.

"Look who's here! The world's greatest paralegal." He gave her a kiss. I try not to watch when my parents do stuff like that, but I could hear their lips smacking. *Ew.*

"It's good to be home. I'm beat," said Mom. Apparently getting to go on a trip like this was a big compliment to her. But it was a compliment that came with a lot of work.

"Did Lauren tell you she got a part in the play?"

"She did, and she was just about to tell me what she was doing with the phone book."

I had forgotten I was holding it. I put it down on the counter. "I'm calling the radio station. I want to ask about a song."

"After a proper greeting," she said. I hugged her again, and then ran to Wai Po's room to let her know that Mom was home, which made me forget about calling the radio station for a few more minutes. Then I did the math I had forgotten about because I had been bumming about Brenda Sue Parker.

Finally I went back down to the kitchen and dialed.

"WTRY." The announcer's voice was low and deep, just the way he sounded on the radio. "Nashville Nick. What can I play for you?"

"Hi," I said. "Um, I was actually wondering if you could tell me who sang a song I just heard."

"That was George Jones with 'You've Still Got a Place in My Heart.'"

"No," I said. "This was a little while ago. It was a woman singing."

"The Judds?"

"Maybe? But there was just one of them."

"Can you tell me how it went?"

"Well." It was really the feeling of the song that got to me.

"Hold on, let me switch to a commercial and we'll solve this mystery." He disappeared and then came back on the line. "Right. So let's hear it: Tell me what you remember about that song."

"Okay," I said. I hummed a little bit and sang the words *lonely* and *blue*.

"That, my friend, is the legendary Patsy Klein, singing 'Have You Ever Been Lonely?' Her music has been around a long time."

Klein! No wonder her music spoke to me. She was Jewish. Like me! And like Calvin Klein, whose name was also on the hiney of designer jeans I didn't own. Patsy probably wasn't Chinese, too. That would be too much to hope for. Still! We had something in common. We were somewhere people weren't expecting us. Also, that meant David was wrong about something, which was always enjoyable.

"This is my first time hearing her," I said.

"Well, just for that, I'm going to play another one for you. So don't touch that radio dial!"

"Thanks, Nashville Nick," I said.

"Call me Nash." Even his nickname had a nickname.

"Thanks, Nash."

"Hey, how about I record you announcing the next song? Just say your name and let everyone know that Patsy Klein's 'Crazy' is coming up next."

I was going to be on the radio! I took a deep breath and thought fast; I needed a nickname, too. Something besides Tara's Friend and The Button Girl and Person Who Will Always Be the Side Dish.

"Hi," I said. "This is Lonesome L! Patsy Klein is coming up next with her hit song 'Crazy.'"

CHAPTER 7

KNOCKOFF

"CRAZY," THE SONG, WAS TOTALLY awesome. It was even more awesome than "Have You Ever Been Lonely?" There was so much emotion in her voice, you didn't want to just sing along, you wanted to cry along, too.

I ran back downstairs as soon as it was over. The kitchen was empty and the lights were off, except for the one over the stove that my mom leaves on as a night-light, in case of emergencies. I wasn't sure what sort of kitchen emergencies there are in the middle of the night, unless you counted midnight snacks. I really wanted a phone in my room, like Tara had.

I dialed WTRY and waited for Nashville Nick to answer.

"It's perfect," I said. "It's a perfect, perfect song."

"I knew you'd like it," he said. "I hope you'll keep tuning in to WTRY." He paused. "That sounded like a commercial, but I do hope you'll keep listening. We play the modern stuff during the day, but at night, I play the real deal."

"I like the real deal," I said.

"Ma'am," said Nash. I wondered if he thought I was really a ma'am, or if he was the type of person who called everyone ma'am. "You have impeccable taste."

"Lauren," Mom called from the living room.

"Thanks again," I told Nashville Nick. I hung up the phone, fast, and ran upstairs and down the hall and jumped into bed.

My mom followed me up the stairs and poked her head into my room. "That's more like it," she said.

I tried to design a Patsy Klein button before school the next morning. I didn't know what she looked like, so I didn't try to draw her. Instead I drew a cowboy hat that ended up looking more like a car. I also tried a horseshoe and a boot. In the end, I just went back to her name, in a turquoise marker, because she sang so much about being blue. That might have been because blue rhymed with so many things: clue, dew, glue, moo, true, woo.

Tara was too nervous to eat lunch before her callback. After school she handed me her peanut butter sandwich and I ate it for her. Sometimes, that is what friends have to do. The other thing they have to do is say "good luck," even if the person they are saying it to never needs good luck.

"I'm going to mess up, I know," Tara said.

She said this before math tests, too, even though she never got below a ninety-six. She said it before she won the science fair and advanced in the oratory contest. But she didn't mess up. Ever.

I didn't know how to respond, so I just squeezed her arm. I stopped squeezing before it turned into a pinch.

I wasn't sure where to sit in the auditorium to watch the callbacks. I thought about sitting in the front, where Tara could see me, and Mrs. Tyndall might see me and realize that she had made a dreadful mistake. I thought about sitting in the back, so I could get out of there as soon as possible.

I ended up picking a seat in the eighth row from the back. I picked the eighth row because there are eight letters in the word *ensemble*, which was where I was hoping Tara would end up so that we could still be We. Then I sat four seats in because there are four letters in *Tara*.

Hector came over and sat down next to me, in the third seat, to wait for his callback. If Mrs. Tyndall was really casting people who looked the part, Hector would be Brenda Sue's dad, the owner of the toy store, because Hector tended to dress like a fussy adult. He liked wearing cardigans and loafers instead of T-shirts and jeans. But wasn't that the whole point of acting? That you could be anything or anyone? That when you stepped into a role, you were transformed? That's how I thought it was supposed to work.

They did the roles of the mayor and Brenda Sue's dad

first. The same two boys, Paul Giardino and Max Burka, who were the tallest boys trying out, had made the cut for both roles. So really it was just Mrs. Tyndall trying to decide who should be who.

"Paul should be the mayor," Hector whispered. "Since he's the SCA president. Audiences like that kind of thing. Connections to real life."

This time, Mrs. Tyndall had them sing the same song, one from the play, so she could compare them. Then she called up Hector and Ricky to sing for the parts of Theodore and Elvis. I noticed Mrs. Tyndall was barefoot. I couldn't tell from the eighth row from the back whether her feet were ugly or not, but in my experience, when adults get to be Mrs. Tyndall's age, feet get pretty unattractive.

"Okay." Mrs. Tyndall swooshed to the center of the stage. "Very nice, boys. Very nice. Now: Where are my Brenda Sues?"

Tara and Jennifer stood up at exactly the same time.

"Lovely," she said. "Let's see. Tara?"

Tara walked slowly up the steps. Her hands were at her sides, like she was fighting to keep them down because the excitement was about to bubble out of her whole body. She was in character.

She sang a song from the musical called "Jumping through Hoops."

She was better than I thought she'd be, though there were still some notes she struggled with. She had these little movements that she incorporated, which told me she had been practicing. She didn't have a Hula-Hoop, but she pretended to have one.

She was adorable and funny. She was wearing a pink oxford, Gloria Vanderbilt jeans, and white sneakers, which made her look just like the girls in the magazines. She wore the smile she had when she was about to come up with a wild-but-good idea. I was so proud that she was my best friend.

And then I wasn't.

Mean, spidery thoughts crept into my brain. Why did Tara get to make callbacks, just because she had blue eyes and freckles? Was there ever, ever anything that she couldn't get? And why couldn't I even have a decent pair of jeans? My mom bought me a pair of knockoff designer jeans from "Sylvia Soupson," who was not a designer I had ever heard of, like Gloria Vanderbilt. Gloria Vanderbilt had a swan on the front pocket of her jeans. Sylvia Soupson had what looked like a pigeon.

I was like the jeans—a knockoff. An imitation of what everyone really wanted.

"I have to go," I mumbled to Hector, who was sitting next to me again. I ran out of the auditorium before Tara, or anyone else, could see how truly terrible I was.

CHAPTER 8

FRIENDSHIP QUIZ

I COULDN'T GO STRAIGHT HOME after school, so I went to Holmes's. They called it a hardware store, but it was really an everything store. Besides hammers and rakes, they carried school supplies, since they were close to the school, and things you couldn't find anywhere else, like egg coddlers. They also sold candy, magazines, bird feeders, crafts, toys, sleds, and rubber ducks with the heads of presidents. And buttons, of course.

At first I grabbed my favorite chocolate bar, which was an Almond Joy, but then I put it back because it reminded me that Tara and I used to sing the jingle together: *Sometimes you feel like a nut, sometimes you don't.* I didn't want anything to do with Tara and singing. I picked out a Zero bar instead and headed over to the magazine rack.

I looked at *Young Miss* and *Seventeen*. They also had *Ms.*, which Tara's mom subscribed to and sometimes made us read. Then I looked at the ones that the high school girls usually got, *Cosmopolitan* and *Glamour*, which had quizzes that told you things like what kind of girlfriend you were and what kind of friend. I opened to a friend quiz.

WHAT KIND OF FRIEND ARE YOU? TRUE BLUE?
OR THE KIND THAT MAKES A GIRL WATCH HER BACK?
TAKE OUR QUIZ AND FIND OUT!

1. Your friend at work gets the promotion that you wanted. What do you do?

A. *Congratulate her!*

B. *Sulk. What does she have that you don't?*

C. *Talk to your boss about why you didn't get the promotion, and work harder next time.*

2. Your friend's car is in the shop, and she wants to borrow yours to run errands on Saturday morning. Your friend is notorious for being late, and you have a blind date at one o'clock. What do you do?

A. *Let her borrow the car! Girlfriends are more important than blind dates!*

B. *No way! There's a reason why her car is in the shop.*

C. *Let her borrow the car, but make it clear that you need the car back on time.*

3. Your friend has you over for dinner, and it tastes terrible! What do you do?

A. *Eat slowly but don't complain. She was being thoughtful!*

B. *Tell her the truth! That's what friends do and besides, you might save someone else from food poisoning.*

C. *Try a compliment sandwich. Find something to compliment (the silverware pattern is nice, right?), then provide some constructive criticism (maybe next time a bit less salt), and close on another compliment.*

I skipped ahead to the scoring section. If you scored mostly *A*'s, you were Sweet and Supportive. Mostly *B*'s meant you were Tough but True. Mostly *C*'s were for friends who liked to Communicate and Compromise. I didn't feel like any of those categories. I needed one of my own: Mad and Sad.

"Buy the magazine or put it back," the clerk called from the register. She was about a hundred years old, with thin hair that looked like wisps of cotton candy.

I put the magazine back on the shelf, and the woman on the

cover stared back at me. All the magazine women stared at me. Three of the covers featured Christie Brinkley, who had long blonde hair, and all the models had blue or green eyes. Not one of them looked like me. It was like the musical all over again.

I walked to the counter with just the Zero bar.

"No buttons today?" asked the clerk.

Now that I had put the magazine back, she was being friendly again and trying to sell me something else.

"Not today," I said. "I'm saving for a pair of designer jeans." I didn't know I was going to say that until the words flew out, but it was true. I was going to have to get my own jeans. Good ones. The clerk looked at the buttons on my jacket. "You probably have enough to start your own button business," she said. She smiled at her own joke.

I thanked her for the Zero bar. I should have thanked her for the idea, too.

Button business.

I had all the equipment. What if I made buttons and sold them at school? I could make them for bands and TV shows and our school mascot. We were the Weimaraners, which was the type of dog Eisenhower had when he was in the White House. Weimaraners aren't very threatening, mascot-wise. But they are pretty cute.

If I had a button business, I'd have my designer jeans a lot sooner. I could save enough for a phone in my room like Tara's, too. Maybe my parents would let me have one if I showed initiative, which is something parents like.

CHAPTER 9

BEATRICE MINERVA

SAFTA, WAI PO, AND BAO BAO WERE
all looking intently into a cardboard box when I came home.
I walked over and took a look.

"A kitten!" I reached down and picked it up. It was soft
and black with white patches on its nose and paws. A tiny
pink tongue appeared when it yawned. "Is it ours?"

"In this house?" Wai Po gave Bao Bao a reassuring
pat. "No."

"She's mine," said Safta. "But what's mine is yours."

"You wanted a cat?"

"I didn't want a cat?" Safta folded up an old towel and
put it in the bottom of the box. "A well-behaved pet is a welcome companion in old age." She gave Bao Bao a look when
she said *well-behaved*.

"Cats don't listen to anyone," said Wai Po. "You'll see."

"Does she have a name?" I asked, hoping to head off an argument.

"Of course she has a name," Safta said. "Beatrice Minerva."

"That's a big name for a tiny cat," I said.

"It is an elegant name for a cat," Safta said. "It's what I would have named your father if he had been a girl."

I decided my father was pretty lucky he'd turned out to be a boy.

I waggled my index finger at Beatrice Minerva, and she attacked it with her two front paws. "I think I'll call her Mini for short," I said. Short for Minerva, but also because she was so tiny. I turned it into a song. "Mini is a tiny cat, a mini cat, a bitsy cat. Mini is my favorite cat. Look at her little paws."

"So . . . Beatrice Minerva comes with a story," said Safta. She paused and looked at me.

"A story? Was someone mean to her?" I held Mini closer to me.

"Not like that," said Wai Po. "A *Let's Make a Deal* kind of story." She harrumphed.

"You make it sound like a bad deal. It's a good deal!" scolded Safta. "The lady giving away the kittens is the sister of my next-door neighbor. She also happens to be the class-mate of my dentist in the city." When Safta says *the city*, she means New York, like it's the only city in the world.

Wai Po rolled her eyes.

"Her name is Helen Mather. Helen was looking for homes for these kittens, and I went to take a look, and she happened to mention that she is opening a T-shirt shop."

"Did you promise to buy a T-shirt if you took a kitten?" Safta was not known for her fashion sense, and I was worried that she was going to make me walk around in a T-shirt that she had designed herself. The last one she gave me said *Jewish American Princess* on the front. There were hardly any Jewish kids at my school, so most people didn't know that Jewish American Princess basically meant spoiled. I don't think Safta knew that, either. The T-shirt stayed at the bottom of the drawer.

"It's the other way around," Safta said. "She was going to give me a free T-shirt if I took a kitten. But I got something better."

"Here it comes," said Wai Po.

"I said, if you're having a store opening on Friday, why not have some entertainment? I have a granddaughter who can sing like nobody's business. She'll get people in your store in droves."

"You promised a lady I've never met that I'd sing in front of her store?" I just wanted to make sure I was getting it right.

"For strangers," added Wai Po. "People who do not know you or your family."

"She's not a stranger; she's Ellen Weber's sister."

"I can't sing there! That's weird. And . . ." I couldn't

say the next words. What if everyone else was like Mrs. Tyndall? They would think I didn't belong there. Maybe they would think I was stupid for singing in front of a store, or worse, stupid for thinking I deserved to sing in front of a store.

"She doesn't even know what I look like," I pointed out. "She might not realize that I'm . . ."

"Beautiful? Sure she does!" said Safta. She reached into her purse and pulled out her wallet. When she opened it, a waterfall of plastic-covered school photos of me and David fell out. "Every year since first grade," she said proudly.

"Mine is longer," said Wai Po. She pulled out her wallet and proved it. "Every picture since kindergarten."

"I have the kindergarten picture in a frame," said Safta.

"What are you going to do when I go to college?" I asked them.

"Get a bigger wallet," said Wai Po. "For graduate school."

Safta got back to business. "To get where you want, you have to find places to sing," she said. "You have to work hard. My father had a pushcart—"

"This would get in the way of her schoolwork," said Wai Po.

"It's after school," said Safta. "On Friday."

"Maybe she doesn't want to be a walking advertisement," said Wai Po. "Selling things."

"Well, that was the deal for Beatrice Minerva," Safta

said. She looked at me. "I might have to take her back if you don't sing."

"No!" I rubbed Mini's soft little ears, and she rubbed her cheek against my finger. "Let me think about it." I knew my safta was trying to help, but this was not what I had in mind.

"Nunu," said Wai Po. That was her nickname for me. "Do not let her make you do something that you do not want to do. But Marjorie is right about one thing. If you want something, you have to work for it."

"I'm right about more than one thing," said Safta.

Right before dinner, the phone rang. It was Tara.

"Are you okay?" she asked. "I thought you were going to stick around for when Mrs. Tyndall made the announcements."

"I forgot I had to do something at home." I swallowed hard. "Did you get the part?" A tiny part of me made a very nice wish for Jennifer, the other girl trying out for Brenda Sue.

There was a long pause. Then Tara screamed, "Yes! I am Brenda Sue Parker! Can you believe it?"

"Congratulations," I said. I thought of the quiz and tried to channel Sweet and Supportive friend. "You'll be great."

"Hector got cast as Theodore. And Jennifer Gallagher's going to play my friend."

"Tubular." It was not a word I normally said. I wasn't sure if that made me sound fake or enthusiastic.

"You would have been tubular, too," said Tara. "But we'll get to be in the play together, and that's what's important, right?"

We. I squinched my eyes shut. "Right."

"Are you sure you're okay? You sound funny."

I wound the cord around my finger. "I'm fine." I tried to think of a distraction. "Safta got a kitten. Her name is Beatrice Minerva, but I'm going to call her Mini."

"I totally need to come see her! I wish I had a kitten." Tara's little brother, Jay, was allergic to dander, so the only pets they ever had were fish, which weren't cute but were calming to look at when they were swimming around. They were not as calming when they were floating at the top of the tank.

"She's mostly black and super soft," I said.

"Aren't black cats bad luck?" Tara said it just like that, almost like she was *wishing* me bad luck. Then her tone changed. "Hey, I was going to ask if you wanted to come to my oratory contest. It's Friday after school. I always feel better when I know you're in the audience. And you wouldn't have to stay long; they're letting me go first since I have to go to my grandma's for the weekend."

This was a thing we did. We were there for each other. But I couldn't watch Tara be good at one more thing. Not this time. Suddenly my decision about the T-shirt shop became easy.

"I'm sorry, I can't. My grandmother booked me a gig on

Friday." I kind of savored the words *booked me a gig*. They sounded grown-up.

"What?" Tara screamed again. "That's amazing!"

I'll be a good friend next time, I promised silently. "It's at the mall," I said. I didn't say it was at the T-shirt shop, so it would sound like maybe it was the whole mall. "It's no big deal."

"Of course it's a big deal! Are you nervous? Are you getting paid? Then you can say you're professional."

I almost mentioned the T-shirt shop. Almost. "It's an opportunity," I said, which was what Safta would have said, too.

"It's an excellency for sure," said Tara. "Kittens and a real singing gig."

It wasn't an excellency. It was an excuse. And now I was stuck with it.

CHAPTER 10

I PITY THE FOD?

I SPENT THE NIGHT MAKING BUTTONS for my new button business. The machine worked a little like a stapler, where you press down to make the pinback and the top part of the button come together. Even though I was making something, the sound and the pressure made me feel like I was destroying something. I thought a lot about Mrs. Tyndall's head.

In the morning, I took some duct tape and attached a long strip of paisley fabric to the inside of my locker door. I had pinned my buttons to the paisley to make a little display. Tara would have been at my locker, normally, but there was a morning meeting for all the people who were oratory finalists. I was on my own.

"What's a fod?" Duncan was using his time before school to possibly become the first paying customer of The Button

Girl, which was what I'd decided to name my business. If you had asked me who was going to be my first customer, I would not have named Duncan, but we were going to be in the ensemble together, so maybe he was trying to be friendly.

"Hunh?" I said.

"'I pity the fod'? What's a fod?"

"It's 'I pity the fool,'" I said. "Mr. T?" The button was at the top of my display. I thought it might make a good button because Mr. T, the guy who originally said it, was popular. He starred on *The A-Team* and wore a Mohawk and gold chains. It was easier for the students at Eisenhower Junior High to copy his language than his fashion sense.

"It looks like you wrote 'fod,'" said Duncan.

I guess the *o* and the *l* were a little close together. But not close enough to look like a letter *d*. "I pity the fool who thinks this says 'fod,'" I said. "If you want it, it's a dollar."

"I'll give you fifty cents," said Duncan. "Because of fod."

I did some calculations. Fifty cents did not give me a very high profit margin. Still, if Duncan wore my button at school, it was a good advertisement. And as a new business, I needed the publicity.

I sang a little bit from Mr. T's song, "Treat Your Mother Right." It's a rap, so it's like half singing, half talking. There's a song for every occasion; this occasion was called Sell Duncan a Button.

Duncan laughed. "You do a pretty great Mr. T!"

"Thanks," I said. "Do we have a deal?"

"Truthfully?" said Duncan. "I can't pay more than fifty cents or I can't buy lunch. I can bring the other fifty cents tomorrow."

Since they were serving fish squares on buns, forcing Duncan to miss lunch might be a favor. But there was always the fruit cup, and I can't stand the thought of people being hungry.

"Fine," I said, taking the Mr. T button off the fabric background. "But you have to tell people where you got it. I'm trying to get this business off the ground." I switched to my Mr. T voice. "Treat your button maker right!"

"Hey," Duncan called out to the first three people who walked past us. "Check it out. Tara's friend is selling buttons. Locker ninety-seven!"

"Great," I said in a cheerful voice. But in my mind, I heard another, unexpected voice. As in, *Great, he only knows Tara's name. Not yours.* "My name is Lauren, by the way. Lauren Horowitz."

"Oh yeah, Lauren, duh, I knew that. I just figured that more people, Lauren, would come if I pointed out that you, Lauren Horowitz, are connected to Tara."

Tara, who was so famous she didn't even need a last name, like Pelé or Cher.

"Okay, ha ha, I get it," I said. It was weird to hear my name said so many times in a row. And Duncan was right about the Tara connection, that it would bring more business, but I didn't want the business to be about Tara. I wanted it to be about me.

Mrs. Tyndall's student assistant saw us and came over. Her blonde hair was pulled up in a high, wavy ponytail, and she wore a blue skirt and pink shirt. "You're that girl who sang Cyndi Lauper," she said.

"Her name is *Lauren*," said Duncan. "Horowitz." He grinned at me, clearly enjoying the fact that he could tease me while seeming like he had good manners. Then he said, "Tiffany Ellison is the stage manager. She just moved here from California. Her natural habitat is the Sherman Oaks Galleria, but she's making the transition to the unique ecosystem of Oak Faire Mall."

"You sound like a scientist." Tiffany play-slapped Duncan, then turned to me. "Oh my god, you were so good. Like, totally amazing. I went home and told my mom you were transcendent."

"That's why I'm in the ensemble," I said.

"A travesty, that's what I say," said Tiffany. "So, are you selling buttons?"

I stood back and showed Tiffany my display. She touched one with her finger. "How much is this one?" It said NOT EVEN.

"They're a dollar each," I told her.

Tiffany reached into her pocket, pulled out four quarters, and handed them to me. "Gotta jet. Mr. Jaramillo is totally averse to tardiness."

"She's from a different planet," Duncan said.

"A planet that buys buttons! I'm okay with that." My mind was recording "gotta jet." I could make that button tonight.

"I'll help get the word out," said Duncan.

Two sales! This was better than babysitting, which paid a dollar an hour. I'd already made $1.50, and I hadn't had to wipe anyone's nose or rear end.

When I got to science, Tara was waiting for me at the door.

"A button business?" she asked. Word got around fast at our school. "You didn't say anything about that last night."

"It's something I just decided to do," I said. *I. Not we.* "To earn money for jeans."

I dug around in my backpack and pulled out the buttons I had made for her. One said ORATORY IS MY CATEGORY. The other had a picture of a black kitten, since she couldn't have one in real life.

"Cool," said Tara. She pinned them to her shirt, so that the kitten button was higher and to the right of the oratory button. Then she pinned them the other way, so the oratory button was higher.

"That one is for good luck," I said. I tried to feel sorry that I wasn't staying after school to watch, and failed. The T-shirt gig was still more appealing. The button would have to do.

"Thanks. Sixth graders never win. But I have to try,

right?" She polished the oratory button with her sleeve. "What do we charge for these circular pieces of art?"

I hesitated. I had wanted the business to be mine, but the thought of saying that out loud seemed mean.

"They're a dollar," I said, relenting. "I have them on display in my locker."

"If I get any interested buyers, I'll show them during lunch." Even though Tara and I didn't have lunch together, we knew each other's locker combinations. We knew everything about each other. "I'll leave you any money on the top shelf. And I'll get to work on new button ideas."

"But I . . ." The bell rang, drowning out the rest of my sentence, which was okay. I wasn't sure how it was going to end.

CHAPTER 11

THE GIG AT TO A TEE

"I'M COMING, TOO," WAI PO SAID when we were getting ready to leave. "For protection." It made her sound like she was in the mob.

"What am I? Chopped liver?" asked Safta. "Why would she need protection?"

"She's singing in front of strangers," said Wai Po.

"Fine." Safta picked up her handbag and swung it onto her arm so it accidentally-on-purpose hit Wai Po in the butt along the way.

Fairfax Carousel Mall was a fifteen-minute drive. The parking lot wasn't crowded, but Safta parked far away, because she liked wiggle room.

The mall had an indoor merry-go-round and an ice cream shop. When I was little, my parents used to take me and my brother there for a ride on the carousel and out for ice cream. The order is important, as we discovered when David once had ice cream before the ride and then threw up in a gigantic circle as the carousel spun around.

To a Tee was on the same side of the mall as the carousel, which was the side the less popular stores were on (not counting the ice cream shop). The store smelled like the inside of a plastic raincoat.

"This is my Lauren," Safta said when we got inside.

"Our Lauren," said Wai Po, introducing herself to Mrs. Mather.

"I see the resemblance," Mrs. Mather said. She gave me the once-over, and I gave her one back. Mrs. Mather looked like she had been in the sun too long; her skin was tan and leathery, but her wrinkles also looked like they came from smiling a lot, which I liked. I wondered which grandmother she thought I resembled. Most of Safta's friends thought I looked "very Chinese," and Wai Po always said that my face was shaped like my dad's, like an oval.

Mrs. Mather had made up a humongous pink T-shirt for me to wear. It looked more like a nightgown, with the words TO A TEE spelled out on the front, surrounded by rainbows, kittens, hearts, and other decals the store would iron on if a customer picked them out. She spray-starched the T-shirt so it was hard and stiff. "It looks like what people think of when they think of T-shirts," she explained. "A perfect T shape."

I hoped, as my bodyguard, Wai Po would protect me

from the T-shirt, but she watched as Safta helped me yank it on over my regular clothes.

"Don't move so much," said Safta. "It will break."

"I'm trying not to let the fabric touch my skin." The shirt was scratchy. It reminded me of the cast I had in fourth grade, when I broke my left arm. Mrs. Mather stuck a pink hat on my head, which I couldn't stop her from doing because I couldn't raise my arms. The front of the hat said ASK ME ABOUT TO A TEE! I wasn't sure how I was going to answer questions from people if I was supposed to be singing, but she was the boss.

"Okay," said Mrs. Mather. "Now go out there and drum up some customers!"

"She is only doing this because of the cat," Wai Po said, but softly, so Mrs. Mather couldn't hear.

"Shouldn't we wait until there are some people out there?" I asked. Even though it was Friday afternoon, the mall was like a ghost town.

"Nonsense! We won't get any people until there's a reason for them to come to the store!" said Mrs. Mather. She handed me a bunch of helium balloons. "Hand these out to little kids. I'll wait in here to make T-shirts."

I walked out to the front of the store, with the balloons and my grandmothers trailing behind me.

There was a shoe store directly across the way, and a vacuum repair shop next door. They were both empty, except for the people working there.

"This seems weird, singing into an empty space," I pleaded

with Safta and Wai Po. "And I thought she would have a song for me to sing. I don't know any songs about T-shirts."

"You don't?" said Safta. "I can't tell what they are singing about in those songs on the radio. There has to be a T-shirt in there!"

"Well, there isn't," I said. Most songs were about wanting someone to love, actually being in love, or mourning a breakup. No T-shirts.

"Maybe you could sing some show tunes," said Safta.

"Show tunes?" said Wai Po, in the voice she usually used to describe Safta's cooking. "Why don't you take the songs from when you were a little girl and put in the word *T-shirt*. That is more appropriate."

"It is not a terrible idea," Safta said, which from her was like saying Wai Po should win the Nobel Prize. "Why don't you start with 'Mary Had a Little T-shirt.'"

"Old MacDonald could also have a T-shirt," said Wai Po.

If Tara had been here, we probably would have come up with something better. I went with Old MacDonald.

> *Old MacDonald had a farm*
> *E-I-E-I-O*
> *And on that farm, he wore a T-shirt*
> *E-I-E-I-O*
> *With a T-shirt here*
> *And a T-shirt there*
> *Here a T, there a T, everywhere a T-shirt*
> *Old MacDonald had a T-shirt*
> *T-I-T-I-O*

"You look like you feel sick," said Wai Po. "We should go home."

"That's just nerves," said Safta. "Try looking happy. You're selling T-shirts! Sing louder!" She said this last part like a command.

I pasted a smile on my face and sang the song again. Louder. This time, the shoe store guy came out of the store and watched.

Safta smiled and pointed at me. "My granddaughter."

Wai Po looked as if Safta had just revealed my secret identity.

"You guys offering any discounts to your fellow mall

employees?" the shoe store guy said. I supposed if Old MacDonald had T-shirts, he would have shoes, too.

Safta grabbed him by the arm. "I'm sure we can work out something. Let's go in!" She steered him into the store.

"Good," Wai Po said. "Now you can take a break."

"I just started," I said. I saw a mom and two kids heading toward the carousel. I wondered if I could get them to come over.

"What should I sing?" I asked Wai Po. They were younger than me, but not so little that they'd like nursery school songs.

"Something respectable," said Wai Po.

Maybe it was because Wai Po was hassling me, but I started singing the "I'm a Little Teapot" song, which would have worked, except that I forgot to actually replace the word *teapot* with *T-shirt*.

I stopped singing the song abruptly, looked down, and threw my arms upward, which was not easy to do in the stiff shirt. "Hey, I'm not a *teapot*! I'm a *T-shirt*!"

The kids, a girl and a boy, came running and gazed up at me in my pink-shirt-and-hat glory. "Your song is funny," said the girl.

I handed each one of them a balloon and pointed at To a Tee. "There's a new store that you can visit. It has lots of different colored T-shirts to choose from, plus decals like this one." I pointed to a kitten on my shirt, which had lots of sparkles.

"I want a T-shirt like hers!" said the little boy. At first I thought he meant the kitten, but then he added, "A big pink one!"

"Her parents have good jobs," said Wai Po, which had nothing at all to do with the color pink.

"Oh, Steven," said the mom. "Boys aren't supposed to like pink!" She said it like it was a law.

"Why not?" I asked.

The mom frowned. "Pink's for girls."

"Pink is for people who like pink," I said. I couldn't believe I was actually saying these words, but they kept coming out. I smiled sweetly. But I didn't feel sweet. Wai Po looked at me and shook her head.

"I love pink," said Steven. "Not bright pink. Like a carnation."

"I like green," said the girl. "All the greens."

"Well, we can take a look," said the mom. She tugged at their hands.

Wai Po waited until they walked away. "You should not have said those things. That's not your business. She is going to think your family did not raise you properly."

I fiddled with the neckline of the T-shirt. "It's just that I'm getting tired of people always talking about *supposed to*, when it's stupid. Like why couldn't he like pink? What would happen if he had a pink shirt?"

"He might get teased at school," said Wai Po.

"But there's nothing wrong with him liking the color pink," I said. "The problem is other people."

Wai Po was quiet for a moment. "I think I understand." She looked around in her purse and pulled out a tube of cream. She began rubbing some into her hands and the smell of cherry almond floated toward me. "When I was a student, I wanted to study physics, but my father wanted me to be a teacher."

It was weird to think of Wai Po as young, but she hadn't been born a grandmother. "What did you do?"

She shrugged. "It ended up not mattering. Mei guanxi. I had to stop my studies during the war."

"Why did you want to study physics?"

"Physics explains things we cannot see," she said. "Gravity, heat, sound, motion. Physics explains why those people can hear you when you sing."

I wondered if there were terms for the unseen forces in middle school. Why were some kids popular and others not? Why was it easier to make friends in elementary school? Why did teachers sometimes seem crabby, even when you were trying to be good?

This thing about physics was a side of Wai Po I had never seen. "Do you miss physics?" I asked.

"Miss? I don't miss it." The way she said *miss* made me think that it didn't mean the same thing to her that it did to me. "But I'm glad I got to study it, even a little."

"Is it weird to grow up during a war in China, and then end up with your granddaughter in a shopping mall with an indoor merry-go-round, singing about T-shirts?" I asked.

"That," said Wai Po, smiling, "is not what I would have guessed would happen."

Maybe that was what happened without *supposed-to*s— the really unexpected.

CHAPTER 12

MOM'S BIG ANNOUNCEMENT

AFTER STEVEN, WE DIDN'T SEE ANY
more kids. But a few adults stopped to listen.

A man tried to give me a dollar, but Wai Po didn't let him. She took the dollar out of my hand and thrust it back at him. "We are not beggars," she said.

"No one thinks we are beggars. He was just trying to be nice," I told her as the man gave Wai Po a strange look. But Wai Po made her mouth into a tight line and shook her head. "I was afraid this was going to happen."

Safta came back after dealing with the shoe store guy. She and Wai Po trailed me as I walked back and forth through the mall. I sang "Row, Row, Row Your T-shirt" and "The Itsy-Bitsy T-shirt." Finally it was time to quit. I tried to lift the T-shirt to get it off.

"It's stuck," I said.

"What do you mean 'stuck'?" said Safta.

"Go out the way you came in," said Wai Po.

"My arms don't bend that way," I said. "No one's arms bend that way." I imagined going through life with a hard, pink outer shell. Beetles did that. Not people.

Mrs. Mather took me into the storage room, and Safta borrowed a pitcher from the people at the ice cream shop and poured water all over me, so the T-shirt would bend. Wai Po yanked it off me, trying to hold it away from my skin so my clothes wouldn't get wet, but I covered up with my wet arms, so it did anyway. I thought Mrs. Mather was going to be mad about having water all over her back room, even though we tried to mop it up with the T-shirt. But she said I could design another shirt of my own, for free, so I guessed she wasn't. I picked a purple shirt and asked if she had a decal with Patsy Klein.

"The singer?" Mrs. Mather wrinkled her forehead. "I have Def Leppard and KISS." Which were bands that sounded nothing like Patsy Klein. I picked a decal with a cat that looked like Mini instead.

Then, right in the middle of pressing the decal on my shirt, Mrs. Mather said, "Your grandmothers are right. You have that something special." She said it very matter-of-factly, like she was announcing that I had a new purple shirt or black hair.

Wai Po and Safta beamed.

"Have you ever thought of going on *Star Search*?" asked Mrs. Mather. "You're as talented as those kids."

"Me?" I said, as if the thought had never occurred to me.

Even though Safta said it all the time, it was different to have Mrs. Mather, who wasn't even related to me, make the suggestion. It made still wanting to audition for *Star Search* seem less foolish. But it turned out, I wasn't the only one who wanted something.

"I'm thinking of going to law school," Mom said at dinner. We had already lit the candles for Shabbat. We had been lighting them more since David's bar mitzvah, and it was normally one of my favorite parts of the week. It was like dividing the week into the part that was everyday and the part that was special. Peaceful. But I didn't feel peaceful about Mom's announcement. I was holding the salad bowl when she said it, and then I wasn't sure if I should pass the bowl or put it down.

"Why would you want to do that?" I said.

I hadn't been thinking about law school. I'd been thinking about Patsy Klein being Jewish and what it would have been like for her family to hear her sing the prayer over the candles in that low, bendy voice. Or the prayer over the challah or the wine. We always went through those prayers pretty fast, but it would have been different in Patsy's house. Neighbors probably gathered around the open windows at sunset, just to hear her. I'll bet if she sang in synagogue on

Saturday mornings, they would get more than old people and kids studying for their bar mitzvahs.

My *why* question did not go over very well.

Wai Po made a gesture, like she was shooing my words away. "Because being a lawyer pays better and is more prestigious!"

"Law school is expensive," my dad said. "Though it would be worth it in the long run. You haven't mentioned this in a few years. Why now?"

"During the trial, one of the lawyers said to me, 'You think about these issues as well as anybody. Did you ever think about going to law school?' It moved the idea back to the front of my mind."

Just like Mrs. Mather and *Star Search*. I wanted to tell Mom that just because people tell you things doesn't mean they're going to happen.

Dad tilted his head to one side. "My wife, the lawyer. That has a nice ring."

"In 1981, Sandra Day O'Connor became the first woman to be a justice on the Supreme Court," said David.

That was just three years ago.

"Maybe you'll be the second," he added.

"My wife, the Supreme Court justice, has an even nicer ring," said Dad.

"I bet the judge on *People's Court* makes more money than the Supreme Court justices," said David.

"Being on TV is not dignified," said Wai Po. "A legal career, that is dignified." She nodded her head approvingly.

"We're getting a little ahead of ourselves." Mom laughed. "We need to figure out finances. I would need to study for the LSAT. And take it. I'd have to figure out where I can apply, though I think some of the partners would write me good recommendations. Law school is three years, longer if I go part-time. And after all that, I'd have to pass the bar exam." Mom ticked each of these items on her fingers.

I looked at everyone else's excited faces and felt like I had failed another magazine quiz on how to be a True-Blue Daughter. Because I thought it was a terrible idea. It was hard enough to get her attention while she was working; it would be twice as hard if she was going to law school, too.

"Lauren?" said Mom.

I dabbed my mouth with a napkin, and spoke mostly into the folds. "I think you wouldn't have much time to be a mom," I mumbled.

"Oh!" Mom jerked back, as if a scorpion had suddenly appeared on her dinner plate. She blinked, one, two, three times.

I felt everyone else at the table glare heat beams of indignation at me. My face turned red, but I didn't feel sorry.

"Your mom is trying to give you the best life," said Wai Po. "You should be grateful."

"No, no," said Mom. "Lauren is just saying what she thinks." But she sounded disappointed.

"If Mom becomes a lawyer, you can have those bogus jeans you've been whining about," said David.

"Not necessarily," said Mom. "The jeans are not just about money; this is about what we value."

"Great," I said. "So I don't even get jeans?"

Dad put his hands up. "Let's not get overheated." He made a patting motion on the air. "This is a new idea. Let's give it time to breathe. Let's all think about it, okay?"

I looked at the candles glowing on the hutch.

What else was there to think about? It seemed like we had said everything that needed to be said.

CHAPTER 13

EN-SEM-BULL

MONDAY MORNING, TARA CAME
running up to me at my locker. "How was your debut professional singing performance?"

I'd helped pull an extra three customers into the store. Most people had just ignored me, which was worse than singing to an empty space. But Mrs. Mather had made that comment about me having something special. I kept that compliment with me all weekend, letting it glow inside me. When we watched *Star Search* that Sunday, I'd paid extra attention to the teen vocalists and started to imagine what I would wear on *Star Search*. Maybe a Gunne Sax dress, if I promised to also wear it for my bat mitzvah.

I didn't tell Tara about the compliment. Instead I pulled out one of the coupons that Mrs. Mather gave me. "It was good. And here. You can get a T-shirt for thirty percent off."

Tara squinted at the coupon. "Oh! It was at the Carousel Mall. I thought it was going to be at Oak Faire." And just like that, the warm glow turned into a cold, black lump.

It was just a stupid thing my grandmother arranged, and not even at the good mall. I got paid in T-shirts and coupons, not real money. Mrs. Mather probably just said what she said to be nice.

"Nope, just good ol' Carousel Mall." I hunted around for something else to say. "My mom says she's thinking about going to law school."

"Whoa," said Tara. "That's kind of huge."

"Yes," I said, relieved that she got it. "My whole family was so rah-rah about it, but no one wanted to talk about how hard it would be."

"I remember when my dad was studying for his exams to become an insurance agent. We hardly saw him."

"Exactly," I said.

"And my mom's still thinking about this mayor thing."

I loved how I never had to explain things to Tara. She just understood. "How was your grandmother's?" I said, putting off the question I was really supposed to be asking.

"Good. She's started a walking club in her neighborhood. They walk three miles a day."

"Did she make chicken piccata?" I knew that was Tara's favorite.

"She made pork chops and mashed potatoes. That's my dad's favorite. Plus apple pie."

If I had my way, I'd stop with my questions there, but there was one more, the question I should have asked first.

"How was oratory?" There. I'd said it.

Now Tara got a huge smile on her face. "I thought I had gone over the time limit, but it turned out I just made it. I totally forgot to say my line about trees and roots, so that helped."

"Who won?" I asked.

Tara smiled. "You'll hear on the morning announcements."

I didn't have to wait for the announcements.

"Congratulations," I said. "That's really great. An excellency." I tried to mean it, even as I could feel the jealousy come back. It settled in my chest like mucus.

The warning bell rang. "See you at practice?" said Tara. It was our first day of real play practice, and not just Mrs. Tyndall handing out forms and going over the rules.

"Yup."

"Save me a seat if you get there first," said Tara.

I got to homeroom in time to hear the principal say, "Congratulations to sixth grader Tara Buchanan, winner of the Eisenhower oratory contest." I pretended to clap along with the rest of the class, but if anyone had looked closely, they would have seen that my hands hadn't actually touched. "Let's wish her luck as she moves on to compete in the county competition!"

I always imagined that middle school musicals involve a lot of busyness. Sets being painted, people learning dance moves, and maybe a teacher rushing onstage to admit that she made a mistake putting you in the background.

But apparently in middle school musicals there is also sitting.

By the time I got to the auditorium, Tara was onstage, talking to Mrs. Tyndall. I looked around for her backpack and found it plopped in a pile with a bunch of other ones. It was not in a seat, the universal sign for "this is saved."

"Hey, Lauren Horowitz. Up here." Duncan was sitting in the last row of seats with a bunch of other kids, who I guessed were also in the ensemble. I climbed up to the second-to-last row and turned around to face them.

"Did I miss anything?" It was nice to have an excuse not to look at the stage, which was radiating the All-American-Girlness that was Tara.

"You missed getting yelled at by Mrs. Tyndall," said

Cheryl Vickers, who was in my PE class. "We can't eat or do homework or read or anything when we're here. Practice time is *her* time. Our job is to pay attention, even when we're not onstage." Mrs. Tyndall probably thought Cheryl also looked like an all-American girl; Cheryl had white-blonde hair and blue eyes. The reason she was in the ensemble and not a starring role, though, was probably because she was also super tall.

"Can't we do something? Like help . . ."

"DO I HEAR NOISE FROM THE ENSEMBLE?" Mrs. Tyndall had turned away from the people onstage and was now glaring at us. I faced forward and slunk down.

Cheryl whispered, "In French, you're supposed to say ensemble." She emphasized the first two syllables: *En-semb*. You could barely hear the *le*. "Mrs. Tyndall says it like she's mad." Plus, she put the emphasis on the *bull* part at the end.

I laughed without making any noise. After a few minutes, I pulled out my Walkman and turned it on. I figured Mrs. Tyndall wouldn't be able to see the headphones from the stage.

Duncan leaned forward and handed me a note.

Boring!

I pulled a pencil out of my backpack.

Boring would be a compliment.

I handed the note back to Duncan. He nodded and added another note.

What are you listening to?

I was listening to a recording I had made of songs from Nashville Nick's show. I'd kept my cassette player next to the radio and managed to tape three Patsys, along with a Dolly Parton song I liked, two by Johnny Cash, and one by Willie Nelson, who, according to Nick, had actually written "Crazy" for Patsy Klein. But you're not supposed to admit to listening to country music, not at my school.

Some stuff I recorded off the radio, I wrote.

I thought it was from the musical. Do you know all the songs yet?

Duncan had nice handwriting. Most boys I knew didn't.

Mostly. Do you? I wrote.

Nope. But you're smarter than me.

I wasn't sure why he thought this. I didn't usually let people see my grades, even in classes I did really well in. *You're smart*, I wrote.

If we're so smart, why are we stuck here?

That was a good question. I passed the note to Cheryl. *Hey, Cheryl, why are we stuck here?* Cheryl wrote something down and then started passing the note around. When it got back to me, there were a bunch of different answers.

Because we are being punished. Cheryl wrote this.

Better than doing nothing at home, wrote Hallelujah Simmons. Her handwriting was strong and clear, like her singing.

I am Russian spy studying habits of American junior high school students! Do not blow cover. I was pretty sure this was from Andy Jenkins, who was in the ensemble but who also had a tiny role as a visiting Russian ambassador, though Andy had talked with a fake Russian accent even before he got the role. He had one line: "We have banned the Hula-Hoop because it is a sign of the emptiness of American culture." He pushed his bangs out of his face, which swooped across the front of his head in a wave. Mrs. Tyndall had already told him that he needed to make his hair look more "traditional" for the show.

We're part of an experiment to see how long we can sit before our butts go numb.

Does anyone have any gum? That was Hallelujah again.

We're not supposed to have gum. Lila Mahoney was kind of a goody-goody. Everything about her seemed squared off and prim, from the bangs that went straight across her washed-every-morning pale face to the light blue cardigan she wore almost every day. Even her handwriting looked like it followed the rules. Then she added, *I bet the leads don't have to wait around for us.* She underlined the last two words.

Aside from Duncan and Cheryl, I really didn't know the kids in the ensemble, but they seemed kind of fun, even if Lila was the Gum Police.

Are we allowed to go to the bathroom? Michael Spiers had to have written this one. Once on a field trip to the zoo, all the buses had to wait while he went to the bathroom one last time. I looked over at Michael, who was sitting with his legs crossed and looking kind of uncomfortable.

"Michael," I whispered. When he looked over at me, I nodded and pointed at the door. He got up and walked out. Mrs. Tyndall didn't say anything. As long as we were quiet, she didn't seem to notice us at all. So when he came back, I left.

I told myself I was just going to go to the bathroom and then come back. But I decided to walk around the school first. It was different without all the other kids there. The hallways were a lot wider than I'd thought. It was super quiet. We'd left a lot of trash behind. I also noticed that the teachers' bathroom, which was usually locked, was partway open.

It was a lot cleaner than our bathroom. When I was washing my hands, I heard a noise behind me like a whisper right behind my ear. What was it? I jumped backward, but I didn't see anyone.

I jogged back to the auditorium.

Mrs. Tyndall was talking about stage left and stage right, which is the direction according to the people onstage. Duncan passed me a note.

Where were you?

Bathroom.

In another building? I must have been gone longer than I thought. Duncan wrote again: *Mrs. Tyndall called for us, but we've been asking her questions to give you more time to get back.*

Not that she would have noticed if I was missing, I thought. *Thanks for covering for me!* I wrote.

No prob.

Mrs. Tyndall turned around to face us. "Is it clear now? The point of the song is to establish that the boys and girls of Pleasant Valley are looking for something new."

"They should visit Mother Russia," said Andy. He was using his Russian accent. Maybe Mrs. Tyndall thought he really was Russian.

"Who is Mother Russia?" asked Lila. "I don't remember her from the cast list."

"It's not a person," said Mrs. Tyndall. "It's a way of referring to the USSR. Sort of like how Uncle Sam means the United States."

"Could Mother Russia date Uncle Sam?"

Mrs. Tyndall took off her glasses and rubbed her eyes. "Let's run through 'Hoopla' with Theodore and Brenda Sue. Ensemble: We'll start with 'Everything Is Still the Same' tomorrow."

Tomorrow? We had spent an entire rehearsal sitting around and hadn't even made it to the stage.

I passed another note. *In real life, side dishes get to be on the table!* I wrote.

"Brenda Sue? Theodore? Last time, from the top," said Mrs. Tyndall.

We listened to them sing one more time before we filed out of the auditorium. Mrs. Tyndall said we would work on singing first, and we would add the Hula-Hooping once we had it down.

Cheryl and Lila came up to me. "What did you mean about side dishes?" said Lila.

I explained about side dishes and main dishes. Cheryl laughed. "I only eat side dishes at Thanksgiving, so side dishes are actually my main dish," she said. "I'm vegetarian."

"I'm never going to look at the ensemble the same way again," said Lila. She started pointing at different people. "Duncan can be mac and cheese. Andy should be borscht. I'll be mashed potatoes. With gravy."

I hadn't chosen my side dish. An apple was too boring. I could say noodle kugel, but no one would know what that was. Or crispy, fried turnip cakes.

Hector and Tara were walking together. "Here come the entrées," said Cheryl.

"Lauren!" Tara threw her arms around me dramatically. "That was intense!"

"Not for the ensemble," I pointed out. "We didn't do anything."

"Not true," said Cheryl. "We sat."

"Oh, trust me, you were lucky." Tara turned to Hector. "When did Mrs. Tyndall say we have to be off book?"

"What does off book mean?" I said. Apparently the leads had learned a secret language while I was in the bathroom.

"It means we have to know all our lines," said Hector. "The speaking parts."

I thought about Duncan and the rest of the ensemble,

and how they had helped me out. Sweet and Supportive friends. True-Blue. We were all in this together, right?

"I could help you memorize lines," I said. "I don't have any speaking parts."

"Lauren is the best," said Tara to Hector. She hugged my arm and rested her head against it.

"The living end," said Hector.

I wasn't exactly sure what that meant, but it sounded like a compliment.

"That's me," I said.

Mrs. Tyndall stood on the stage and looked up at the lighting booth. "We're done for the day," she said. "Turn on the ghost light." A tall light that I hadn't noticed before came on.

"What's that?" I asked.

Mrs. Tyndall seemed pleased by my question. "It's a theater tradition," she said. "You leave a light on when you're done for the day."

I wondered if they did that just for theater productions, or when we used the auditorium for things like PTA meetings and spelling bees.

"What does the ghost part mean?" I got a cold back-of-the-neck feeling and made a mental note to tell Tara about it. Tara claimed that she had seen a ghost in the cemetery on the way home from her grandmother's house. No one in her family believed her. I believed Tara, even though I wasn't sure what Jewish people were supposed to think about ghosts. Wai Po once told me there was a ghost month in China.

"Some people think theaters are haunted," Mrs. Tyndall said. "Ghost lights keep the ghosts company so they won't pull any tricks. Other people think that it's a good safety device so that no one is stumbling around in the dark."

"What do you think?" asked Tara.

"I think it's a good idea not to go against theater tradition," said Mrs. Tyndall.

Tara and I traded an excited glance. The Royal We was definitely interested in ghosts!

CHAPTER 14

NOT *WEIRD*-WEIRD. JUST DIFFERENT.

WE DECIDED TO PRACTICE AT MY house the next day. That way, Hector could hang out with my brother after we finished. He came over with his hair slicked back, instead of parted in the middle and flipped back. Also, he was wearing a navy-blue cardigan with white arms and a giant letter *F* above the pocket. The *F* was orange.

"What's that stand for?" I said.

"University of Florida," he said. "It was my uncle's. Nobody from my family went to school in Pleasant Valley, Tennessee, or a school that begins with *P.*"

"There was a war between ranchers in Arizona called the Pleasant Valley War," said my brother, David. "There are two places in Virginia called Pleasant Valley." David had hung out at our rehearsal, even though he didn't have a role. Apparently this was what he spent his time thinking about.

"Is that your costume?" I asked.

"Nope," Hector said. "I thought it would help me get into character."

David nodded. He had seen enough of Hector's schemes to know when to go along with them. "Does that mean we have to call you Theodore now?"

"Only outside of school," he said. "Otherwise people would think it was weird."

People already thought Hector was weird, but I did not point this out.

"Theodore and Brenda Sue become boyfriend and girlfriend during the show," said David.

Hector turned bright red. "It's pretend. Not like you and a certain person."

Hector was thinking about Kelli Ann Majors, a girl my brother had a crush on. He'd even danced with her at his bar mitzvah, but as far as I knew, that was as far as things had gone. She had two small roles in the play, as Elvis Presley's publicist and as one of the town moms.

"Maybe you should carry her books," David said. "Didn't they do that in the fifties?"

"Hmm," said Hector.

"Do you kids want a snack?" asked my dad. He was working a late shift tonight and hadn't left yet.

"What foods were popular in 1958?" Hector asked. "I think I should adjust my diet accordingly. At least until the play."

"That was the year I graduated from high school," said my dad. "All I remember is drinking Tang and eating a lot of frozen peas."

Tara came in, and we went upstairs to drop off our backpacks. When we came back, my dad was showing Hector how to make a grilled peanut butter and banana sandwich. It was Elvis's favorite food, according to my dad, so Hector deemed it appropriate to eat, even though Ricky was the one playing Elvis. Casseroles were also popular in 1958, but there wasn't enough time to make one.

"Back when I was eating these, I thought they tasted best with root beer," Dad said. He opened four cans of root beer and gave them to us. He was right. The spiciness of the root beer was a nice contrast with the sweet banana and the salty peanut butter.

"Root beer has been around since the 1800s," David said.

That made me think of the ghost light. "Do you think that the school theater could be haunted?" I asked.

"No," David said.

"Why not?"

"Because there's no such thing as ghosts," he said.

"But not everything has a rational explanation," said Hector.

"The theater has a ghost light," Tara told my dad. "They all do. They have to be there for *some* reason."

"Because they don't want anyone to trip in the dark," said David.

"Have you ever heard of someone dying in the Eisenhower Junior High Theater?" I asked. Dad worked in a hospital, so it seemed like he would know.

"Dying *tragically*," said Tara.

"Ah," said Dad. "Sorry, I've got too much going on in the real world to worry about the spirit world."

I took another bite of sandwich. "Why haven't you made this before?" I asked. It was way better than regular peanut butter and jelly.

Dad shrugged. "I haven't thought about grilled peanut butter and banana sandwiches in years—not until Hector reminded me."

"This is weirdly good, Mr. Horowitz," said Tara.

"Yeah. Thanks, Big Daddy," Hector said. "These are gangbusters."

After we finished our sandwiches, we went up to my room, where I had pictured Tara and me practicing together when I thought we might both get leads.

In the first scene that she's in, Brenda Sue describes why she likes Theodore to everyone in the school cafeteria. She's supposed to be all dreamy and in love, but Tara kept laughing.

"Can you imagine saying this in the middle of the cafeteria?" she said. "'Theodore may be an egghead with an overbearing mother, but I love him.' What teenager would say that?"

"You have to have a motivation," I suggested. "We'd say 'nerd.'" Out of the corner of my eye, I saw Hector's face twitch. He and David were the nerd kings at our school. This year they'd been hanging out with Scott Dursky, who was on the cool side, but it hadn't rubbed off.

Tara read her line again. This time she let out a loud hiccup. She covered her face. She took a deep breath and made her shoulders go up and down.

"It's a tough line because she's conflicted," said Hector.

"Let's just skip that part for now. You just need to know the words—you don't need to do all the emotions." We read a few more lines. I coached her. "Then you leave the cafeteria. What's your next line? See . . ."

"See you later, Imogen. Oops. *Hic*. Want to get a soda after school?" Tara said Imogen with a hard *g*.

Imogen was being played by Jennifer Gallagher, the other girl who had made the finals for Brenda Sue.

"It's a soft *g*. Like *giraffe*," I said. "*Imma-jen*. Not *I-mo-geen*, like in *green*."

"It's from Shakespeare," added Hector.

"But this. *Hic*. Isn't Shakespeare." She shouldn't have had that root beer before practice. Tara tossed down her script. "I can't focus with these hiccups. And Imogen's a weird name! It sounds like that tummy medicine."

"Imodium?"

"Yes! Can't we just change it to something easier, like Jen?"

"We can say it," Hector pointed out.

"Well, yeah. You guys are used to saying weird stuff!"

"What's that supposed to mean?" I wasn't sure how Hector and I had become *you guys*.

Tara stood up and took a deep breath of air and held it. When she was done, the hiccups were gone. "I mean, Hector speaks Spanish, and you have your middle name," Tara said.

My middle name is Le Yuan, which sounds nothing like Imogen. My grandfather picked it so it would sound sort of like Lauren. David's middle name is Da Wei—same deal. "Are you saying my middle name is weird?" I said.

"Not *weird*-weird. Just different." Tara wrinkled up her face. "Don't be mad. I know I don't ever say it the right way, that's all."

Here's the thing—I didn't share my middle name with a lot of people because no one *ever* said it the right way. But I had told Tara because we were best friends.

"Thanks a lot," I said.

"You're the one who doesn't even write down her middle name on the school forms," said Tara. She turned to Hector. "She always writes down *L*."

"Because no one gets it right," I said.

"Which kind of proves my point," said Tara.

"Are you guys fighting? Aren't you supposed to be best friends?" Hector said.

Supposed to, I thought.

"We're not fighting," said Tara. "Besides, Lauren is the one who's mad, not me."

"I'm not mad," I said.

"You're doing that thing with your mouth," said Tara.

"For the record, being able to speak Spanish is not the same as saying weird stuff," Hector said.

"I didn't mean weird! Not in the way you guys are making it out to be! I meant it as a compliment. You don't even have to think when you see the name *Imogen*; you just say *Imogen*." This time, she said the name correctly.

I knew Tara meant what she said, that she meant it as a compliment, and that as a True-Blue friend, I should take it as one. But it didn't make me feel good. It just made me feel different.

CHAPTER 15

MINI ON THE TOILET

THE NEXT DAY WE HAD DINNER AT
Safta's house. I went into the bathroom to wash my hands.
The sink was the color of mint chocolate chip ice cream,
only without the chips. The toilet was that color, too, and
on it I found . . .

Mini!

I yelped. Mini stared at me, flicking her tail but not
moving off the seat. Safta ran down the hall. She made a lot
of noise, even though she was wearing tennis shoes.

"Don't shout! I'm training Beatrice Minerva."

"Training Beatrice Minerva to do *what*?"

Safta motioned for me to follow her back into the hall.
"A lady needs her privacy."

I looked at Mini. "Why?"

"To do her business," Safta said.

I leaned back so I could peek through the doorway. Now that I looked more carefully, I could see that Mini was sitting on a clear plastic circle with a small hole cut out of the middle.

"It's more sanitary than a litter box," said Safta. "I saw a commercial for it on TV. Every week, I just cut the hole in the circle a little bigger, until she's used to the toilet seat."

"That's . . ." I was going to say "weird."

"Better than picking up after a certain dog," said Safta. "And it's better than having litter all over the floor, too."

"Cats aren't supposed to—" I stopped myself. "Whoever thought a cat could use a toilet?" I asked.

"Someone who got tired of cleaning out litter boxes," said Safta. "A very smart someone."

"Don't you worry about her falling through the hole?" I asked. "She's so little."

"It isn't like the deep end at the pool," said Safta. "And cats can swim."

"I bet whoever came up with it got laughed at a lot," I said.

She shrugged. "You should always be willing to laugh at yourself, but others? *Psssht*. Forget about 'em."

I thought that would be easier to say once I was out of junior high.

Mini hopped off the toilet seat and strolled out of the bathroom with a sharp meow. Safta picked her up. "Such a good girl, Beatrice Minerva!"

I wondered if Safta's Jewish geography—her ability to make a connection to any Jewish person in the world through her dentist, her favorite bagel shop, or her cousin's mother-in-law's best friend—could work its magic for Patsy Klein. Safta always said she knew someone who knew someone.

"Do you know of any Jewish people in country music?" I asked as we headed to the dining room.

"Let me think about it." But Safta seemed to only be thinking of Mini. "Beatrice Minerva used the toilet like a nice, clean kitty," she announced.

"Did she flush?" asked Dad.

"We haven't gotten to that part yet," said Safta.

"You're an amazing kitty, Mini," said Mom. She didn't pet Mini, because she had already washed her hands. She was sitting next to Dad and across from David. I couldn't prove it, but it felt like she was avoiding me. I took the seat next to David. Safta sat at the head of the table. A brisket with carrots and potatoes was in the middle of the table.

"Bao Bao is also amazing," said Wai Po, who sat at the other end of the table. She had packed her own plum sauce to put on the brisket, even though the flavors didn't necessarily go together. "He just isn't a show-off. The other day, he found one of my shoes."

"You mean he was eating one of your shoes," teased my dad.

"How else is he supposed to carry a shoe? Between his paws?" asked Wai Po.

Even though he wasn't there to hear these insults, I felt bad for Bao Bao. He was used to being the entrée, but now he was a side dish, too.

"It's all a matter of expectations," said Safta. "High expectations for good behavior." Suddenly she clapped her hands together and shouted, "Nudie Cohn!"

For a second, I thought it was one of Safta's sayings, like *keinehora* or *oy gevalt*. But it turned out that she hadn't forgotten about my question.

"Nudie Cohn is a friend of your grandpa Joe's cousin Artie Lipsitz," she explained. "He's in country music, but he's not a singer. He makes costumes. He made one for Elvis and lots of stars. Nudie suits, they're called."

"Nudie suits?" David nearly spit out his food, and everyone at the table went on high alert. Ever since the Thanksgiving choking incident, we've been careful to pay more attention to such things. "Like naked?"

"His real name is Nuta Kotlyarenko. It's Ukranian."

I was disappointed that Safta did not have a connection to the Kleins, but at least she had one to somebody. Expectations were a funny thing. I had asked my question because I believed in Safta's Jewish geography. But sometimes expectations kept people from doing things, like Wai Po from studying physics. And sometimes they got people—or cats—to try new things, like using the toilet. Mrs. Tyndall hadn't cast me because she thought I wasn't what people were expecting. I didn't know how to change any of that, the good or the bad.

Maybe there was a song for these feelings. Patsy probably had one. Was there a word for not knowing if trying a new thing was good or bad? If I should keep trying to make good things happen? I didn't know it, but I knew who did.

When we got home, I got the phone and dragged it into the bathroom. I dialed and waited.

"Nashville Nick on WTRY. What can I play for you?"

"Hi, Nash. It's Lonesome L."

"How is the world's newest Patsy Klein fan?"

I twirled the cord around my finger. "That's a tough question."

"Well, I'm sorry to hear that." He really did sound sorry, which made me feel better.

"I was thinking a new Patsy song might make me feel better." I paused. "Nothing is going like I expected right now."

"Let me think." Nash made a clicking noise with his tongue. "This seems to call for an extra-special Patsy song. I think I'm going to dig into my vault and find her duet with Bobby Lord."

"A duet?" I thought of Tara. Of "Winter Wonderland."

"Sure. This was a song that someone suggested, and Patsy and Bobby sang it together on the spot. They weren't expecting to do that, and the song turned out great. It's called 'Remember Me.'"

Patsy's voice was so beautiful, it was hard to imagine it with anyone else's. But I was willing to try anything. "Okay."

"You'll have to give me a few minutes. I don't play this song very often, but I think you'll love it."

It took Nash five songs to find "Remember Me." I imagined him running back and forth between the shelves and the turntables, keeping the music playing while he looked. "Remember Me" starts with just Patsy, and then the other singer joins in, and they take turns singing alone and together. When Patsy sang with Bobby Lord, her voice seemed sweeter, like the middle of an Oreo cookie against the deeper flavors of the chocolate wafers. I closed my eyes and let myself float on the sound.

I called Nash back after the song was over. "Thanks," I said.

"Thank you for reminding me that song was there," said Nash.

"When I hear Patsy, I don't feel like my problems are solved, but at least someone understands them," I said.

"Sometimes that's all we need in this world," said Nash. "At least for a while, to tide us over."

CHAPTER 16

VINCENT CHIN

A FEW NIGHTS LATER, MOM BROUGHT
home a course catalog from a law school. She showed it to us at dinner.

"Look at all these classes!" She thumbed through the pages the way some kids looked at the Sears Wish Book.

The class names made no sense to me. What was civil procedure? And weren't torts a kind of cake?

"Why would you want to take all those classes?" I said. "They look boring." Wai Po shook her head at me.

Mom put the catalog away.

"You should tell her," said Dad. "About Detroit."

Mom lifted an eyebrow. Even though my dad had only said the word *Detroit*, it seemed like he had a specific story in mind. I hated it when my parents talked like this, in code.

Mom sighed. "You know how Detroit used to make a lot

of cars?" she said. Why was she talking about cars? We nodded, and she went on. "The city has really been struggling. One of the reasons is that more people are buying cars from Japan and Europe."

I had seen bumper stickers that said BUY AMERICAN. THE JOB YOU SAVE MAY BE YOUR OWN. David and I nodded again, and Mom kept talking. "A few years ago, there was a Chinese man named Vincent Chin. He was about to get married, so he went out with his friends for a bachelor party. He lived in Detroit."

I still wasn't sure what this had to do with anything, but she kept talking. "Two auto workers who had lost their jobs saw Vincent Chin at a nightclub. They thought he was Japanese, and they got into a fight. They were all thrown out, but the two men went looking for Vincent. They found him." She looked at my dad to see if she could keep going. Safta and Wai Po looked at their hands.

"One held him down while the other one beat him with a baseball bat," she finished.

David made a tight noise in his throat. Wai Po covered her eyes. Mom took a drink of water.

"Did he survive?" asked David.

"No," said Mom. "He didn't. They buried him on his wedding day."

"What happened to the men?" David asked. "They're in prison, right?"

My mother shook her head. "The judge said they didn't seem like the kind of men who should go to prison."

"No justice," said Wai Po. "Those poor parents."

"Vincent Chin should have told them he was Chinese, not Japanese," I said.

"That's not the point," said Mom. She turned to Dad. "I think Lauren might have been a little young for that story."

If there was one thing I hated more than my parents talking in code, it was talking about me like I wasn't there.

"David wasn't too young," Dad pointed out. "And he's only a year older."

Comparing me to David was strike three.

"May I be excused?" I asked. I stood up before anyone could answer.

CHAPTER 17

TUNES BEFORE HOOPS

I TRIED NOT TO THINK ABOUT Vincent Chin, but he became like a ghost in my head, darting in and out. Even during my classes, it seemed like he was there. It wasn't until I got to rehearsal that something else filled my brain. The songs and dance steps blotted out everything else.

When the ensemble finally got onstage to rehearse, Mrs. Tyndall decreed that we would not move on to Hula-Hoops until we achieved the proper sound. "You indicated on your forms that you were at least at an intermediate level in your Hula-Hooping skills, so I've decided to focus on singing for now," she said.

We'd all seen the Hula-Hoops backstage in stacks. It seemed a waste not to use them, but no one was going to argue with Mrs. Tyndall.

Duncan, Andy, and Max Burka, who was playing Brenda's dad and who was also in my Hebrew school class, called me over after Mrs. Tyndall made her announcement.

"What's up?"

Duncan looked at Andy, who looked at Max. I thought maybe they were going to ask me to ask Cheryl if she liked Andy as a friend or more than a friend, since Andy always sat next to Cheryl during rehearsals.

But Duncan scratched his neck. "How long does it take to learn how to Hula-Hoop?"

I looked at them. "You don't know how to Hula-Hoop?"

"I know how to solve the first two layers of the Rubik's Cube," said Andy defensively.

"I can do a kickflip on my skateboard," said Duncan.

"I can almost moonwalk," said Max.

"The name of this musical isn't *Watch Me Moonwalk, Kickflip, and Solve Two-Thirds of a Rubik's Cube*," I said. "It's about Hula-Hooping."

"The last layer is much harder than the other two," Andy said.

"Obviously," said Duncan. "'Cause then you'd solve it."

"How'd she let you in if you were beginners?" I said.

"I said I was advanced," said Andy.

"Me, too," said Max.

"I don't remember what I put," said Duncan. He looked slightly embarrassed, probably because at this point, my mouth had fallen open into a large, round O.

"You lied?" I said.

"It was not lie," said Andy in his Russian accent. Then he switched back to his American one. "I *could* be advanced if I actually Hula-Hooped."

"But you didn't know how when you tried out," I said. "I *know* how to Hula-Hoop, and I only put down intermediate." Now I was kicking myself for not putting down advanced.

"Will you help us?" asked Duncan.

"You'll probably be fine," I said. "I heard that Mrs. Tyndall is bringing in a Hula-Hoop expert to teach us some tricks."

"Please," said Duncan.

"How bad are you?" Hula-Hooping was like reading for me. I knew that at one point in my life I couldn't do it, but I couldn't remember what that was like anymore. And I wasn't sure how to teach it.

Duncan motioned for me to follow him backstage. He picked up a hoop from the forbidden stack. "This will only take a second." Duncan spun the hoop around his waist. The hoop spiraled one, two, three times before clattering to the ground.

"You need to move your hips," I told Duncan.

"I did," said Duncan.

Andy and Max also took turns. It didn't seem possible, but they were worse than Duncan.

"Have you actually even seen someone Hula-Hoop before?" I asked. "You're supposed to try to keep the hoop around your body, not on the ground." I picked up a hoop and showed them. "You have to find a rhythm."

"So will you help?"

I was tempted to say no. But then I remembered how they had all bailed me out that day when I was wandering around instead of being at rehearsal. "Well—"

"G—" Duncan froze. His eyes grew wide.

"What?" I stood still and lowered my voice. "Ghost?"

Duncan pointed behind me with a single finger. I turned around to see Mrs. Tyndall instead, which made it twice as disappointing.

"I thought I heard something," she said. "I also thought I had made it pretty clear that members of the ensemble had not yet earned the right to use the Hula-Hoops. Only the leads may use them."

I stepped out of the hoop and quietly put it back on the pile. It wasn't fair; the boys had also been using the hoops— they were the whole reason I even had one—but she wasn't looking at them. She was only looking at me.

"Mrs. Tyndall, Lauren was just—" Duncan started.

She put up her hand, stopping him. "I'm quite aware that Lauren is dissatisfied with my casting choice. I suppose she's looking for ways to show off."

What? I wasn't showing off. My whole body buzzed. The

worst part was that Mrs. Tyndall didn't even sound mad. She sounded like she pitied me for even harboring the foolish idea that I could have been cast as Brenda Sue. *I pity the fool.*

I looked at Duncan out of the corner of my eye. He was shaking his head very slightly.

I made up my mind—I'd help the boys. Not because they totally deserved it. And not because Mrs. Tyndall deserved a perfect show. But it was us against her. I wasn't a show-off, but I had news for Mrs. Tyndall: The ensemble was going to steal the spotlight.

First we had to get the singing right.

I thought about Patsy Klein and Bobby Lord singing together. They hadn't even planned it, and they sounded so beautiful together. They also sounded like they meant the words of the song—remember me, I'm the one who loves you when everything else goes wrong. I passed around a question to the ensemble when we got to our seats.

What are you thinking about when you sing "Everything Is Still the Same"?

Dinner

Homework

How everyone sounds better than me

I think about my grandma because she used to sing to me.

I wonder why I can't think of the words ahead of time, but then I can sing them at the right time.

How to get to the next level in Ms. Pac-Man

I thought maybe half the group would feel the same way

I did—that the song was about wanting things to be different, about how sameness can be comforting and a trap at the same time. But maybe I was the only one.

So I wrote: *We need to pretend that we're the people in the song. We're bored kids in a small town who want something NEW.* I passed the slip of paper again.

Like the space shuttle?

The Olympics!

Poor kids, all they have to look forward to is a Hula-Hoop.

Yeah, they should have had Nintendo.

I could have had a V8.

I circled the word *pretend* and drew an arrow to an empty spot on the paper, where I wrote, *Imagine living somewhere where it's really hard to see something new. Imagine seeing the same people your whole life. Imagine being told that a Hula-Hoop is dangerous.*

The paper went from hand to hand. No one wrote anything until the paper got to Lila. She wrote, *Is that what you think about when you sing?*

I wrote: *I pretend to be the person who would need to sing the words.*

Every person in the ensemble looked at me, and I looked each person in the eye to make sure they understood. Every person probably had their own version of what I was talking about. Maybe each person felt some different proportion of angry, bored, and a little scared, but now we were closer to being together.

"Okay," Mrs. Tyndall said, tapping her cane on the floor. "Let's hear it."

We walked over to our places and sang. We didn't sound perfect, but we sounded better. We had that underbelly of feeling you need to make a song sound real.

I looked at Mrs. Tyndall. In my head, I dared her to keep the Hula-Hoops away from us much longer.

CHAPTER 18

A BIG ORDER

THE NEXT MORNING TARA WAS
waiting for me at my locker, like always. "I got us a huge
order of buttons," she said.

"You did?" I still wasn't sure how I felt about the *us* part
of my button business. But most things were better with the
Royal We. And my part of the Royal We didn't have any
family members who were running for mayor. Tara's part of
the Royal We did.

"She officially decided," Tara said. It was like my mom
just deciding to go to law school. "She needs name recogni-
tion, and I suggested buttons. Guess who's making them?"

"Us?"

"The leads have extra practice this week," Tara said. "So
maybe you should handle this one."

I tried not to feel annoyed. "How many buttons are we

talking about here?" It was a job for *us*, but *I* was the one who was going to do all the work.

Tara's eyes twinkled the way they did right before she delivered good news. "A hundred!"

"A hundred!" I did some quick math in my head.

"You can get your jeans." Tara went over the details. All the buttons had to be in red, white, or blue. They had to say "Buchanan for Mayor" or just "Buchanan."

"When does your mom need them?"

"She has a breakfast on Saturday morning, so she wants them on Friday night."

"Friday night!" That meant I had to make twenty to twenty-five buttons a night after practice and homework. I thought about the jeans. "I can do it."

"You can, totally," said Tara. "You can repeat patterns. It's not like you have to make a hundred unique buttons. And if she wins the primary, she'll probably want more."

I had been a little upset with Tara since the whole middle-name business, even though I had been trying to let it go. This helped.

"Thanks. This is totally an excellency! A designer jeans ex-cell-en-cyyyyy!" This time I sang it out.

It felt like we were back to the easy way of being friends. I crossed my fingers and hoped it would stay that way.

The day after the ensemble ruled on "Everything Is Still the Same," Mrs. Tyndall said we could bring out the Hula-Hoops.

We made it through half a rehearsal before: "Vatch this," Andy said in his Russian accent. He dove through a hoop as Michael rolled it across the floor, and crashed, face first, into a chair.

"Nothing, this is nothing," he said as blood dripped out of his nose. He wiped it on the back of his hand.

"Maybe Andy will become the ghost of the theater," said Cheryl. "Woooooo." Everyone laughed, except Mrs. Tyndall.

"Injuries are not a laughing matter," she said as Tiffany left to get an ice pack. "We are professionals. We need to be able to control ourselves. And our hoops. We have lost important play time due to an injury." She was using the royal we. Then she said, "I don't have this problem with the leads."

Mrs. Tyndall hooked her cane around Andy's hoop and lifted it up. Now it had a sharp point on one side.

The ensemble stood on the stage in a guilty circle.

"You," Mrs. Tyndall said, pointing a bony finger toward the auditorium. "Come here."

Everyone's head swiveled around to see who she was talking to. David looked up from his book. "Who, me?"

I think David had just assumed that Mrs. Tyndall would never notice him hanging out at play practice. We had silently agreed not to acknowledge each other's existence when we were at school. Though I might speak up if he suddenly needed a kidney or something.

"Yes." Mrs. Tyndall waited for David to walk up to her.

I could tell David was nervous because he kept tugging at his shirt.

"You are here a great deal for someone who has no responsibilities with the play," said Mrs. Tyndall.

"I'm just waiting for Hector," said David. And Kelli Ann, I silently added. Kelli Ann, whose lines as Elvis's publicist in the play consisted of, "Did someone in this town ask for a hip shaker?" and "Right this way, Elvis." Her mom character was a member of Mothers United for Decency, so she also frowned a lot and made comments about her children.

"Well, I need a hoop wrangler," said Mrs. Tyndall. "Do you want the job? Otherwise, I am going to ask you to leave the practice. It really is only for students involved with the play."

"Okay?" Then David asked what we were all thinking. "What's a hoop wrangler?"

"The hoop wrangler is in charge of making sure that the hoops are ready for rehearsal and are not used for any offstage shenanigans. You bring the correct hoops on for the scene we are rehearsing, and you collect them immediately afterward. If any hoops are damaged or broken, you need to let the props manager know immediately."

David nodded. "Seems pretty simple."

"It is exceedingly simple. But what I need is a perfectly simple job performed with pimple serfection."

The whole room exploded in laughter. David turned red,

even though he wasn't the one who said it; maybe because it's the sort of thing he would usually say.

"Settle down," said Mrs. Tyndall. "You know what I mean." Though she smiled a tiny bit.

After we got back to our seats, Duncan whipped out a piece of paper. He wrote, *Pimple Serfection sounds like an acne treatment.*

Better than pimple infection, I wrote. We passed the paper around.

Gross.

Pimple surf-action?

Clearasil. That's the way to go.

Pimple serfection is another sign of American decadence. That was Andy.

Did I miss something? Michael, of course.

HULA-HOOPING REQUIRES *Circular Reasoning*

After Andy got his bloody nose under control, Mrs. Tyndall introduced the Hula-Hooping expert that she had promised. That expert was Tiffany, button purchaser, fetcher of ice packs, and stage manager. It turned out that Tiffany was the San Fernando Valley Hula-Hoop Champion of 1982. She was wearing a white leotard with matching tights and baby-blue leg warmers, with a matching headband. She looked like the women on TV who did perfectly synchronized aerobics. I did not think this outfit was necessary for Hula-Hooping, but apparently I was wrong.

Some of the eighth-grade boys who worked in the lighting booth in the back of the auditorium stopped to watch. And laugh.

"Okay. So. The first move we're going to work on is the catch and swirl," said Tiffany. She demonstrated by doing a few hoops before swiftly catching the hoop in her hand and continuing the motion up. She made it look easy. It was not.

Max, Andy, and Duncan had not improved much, even though I had told them to practice whenever they could. They could not do the catch and swirl because you needed to be able to do a basic hoop first so that you had something to catch. Tiffany stopped to watch them.

"We have an impending issue here," she said. "Most imminent."

The lighting booth boys laughed harder. One of them stabbed at a button on the panel, making the ghost light flick on and off. "Look," he said. "Special effects."

"The lighting crew will be respectful," said Mrs. Tyndall, thumping her cane for emphasis. The light turned back off.

"Hey," Tiffany said to David. "You're going to have to, like, make some adjustments as the hoop wrangler."

The lighting booth boys were still laughing. "*Like*, um, is like my favorite word," said one of the boys, mocking Tiffany.

Tiffany pointed her perfectly polished fingernail at Max, Andy, and Duncan. "You need to adjust the hoop size to the person. If the circumference is too small, you need to work harder to keep the hoop up. Also, do you have any weighted hoops? That will slow down the rotation and make hooping easier."

"I—I think I have different sized hoops?" said David. It was not a bad answer given that he had only had his new job for five minutes.

"You should also consider wrapping some of the hoops with gaffer's tape. You have that, right? You'll make the hoops less slippery, and the increased friction will make it easier for the guys to keep hooping. Like you totally can't work with two slippery surfaces and expect any traction."

"Got it," said David.

The boys in the lighting booth stopped laughing and got back to work. But I had to admit, I had underestimated Tiffany, too.

"The maximally important thing, though? You have to practice," said Tiffany. "Promise you'll practice, okay? You need to develop muscle memory so that you don't have to think when it's time to perform."

They mumbled okay, and Tiffany smiled and went back to demonstrating different moves. The elevator, where the hoop moves up and down the body. Isolations, which make the hoop look like it's practically floating and spinning in place. Hand spins. It was a lot to take in.

At the end of the practice, Tiffany looked up at the lighting booth. She'd been acting like she hadn't heard the boys making fun of her, but it was clear that she had.

"Hope you enjoyed learning some new moves," she said sweetly. "I was San Fernando Valley Hula-Hoop Champion in 1982." She paused. "Because I was San Fernando Valley Science Fair Champion in 1981."

CHAPTER 19

THE ROYAL SHE

DAVID TOOK HIS ROLE AS HOOP wrangler seriously. He figured out who should have what size hoop, and asked people if they wanted grip tape. He also checked the hoops before and after practice for warping and damage.

"I think you're getting a *little* carried away," I told him after he'd been on the job for a few days. I snagged Tara as she walked by. "Don't you think that David's getting a little too involved in this hoop wrangler business?"

David stood up a little straighter. "It's actually an important job. I just found one of the hoops in the lighting booth."

"Maybe the theater ghost put it there," I said.

"Maybe one of the lighting guys was inspired by Tiffany and borrowed a hoop without asking." He turned to Tara. "Your wooden hoop should be coming in tomorrow."

As Brenda Sue, Tara had a song called "Circling through Time," where she sang about the ways children played with hoops all over the world through the centuries. Mrs. Tyndall didn't want one made of plastic, like all the rest, and had arranged to get a wooden hoop instead. It was Tara's big solo for the show, with a spotlight and everything.

"Thanks," said Tara. "Make sure no one touches it, especially those dimwits in the ensemble. I don't want one of them to break it."

Dimwits in the ensemble?

"You got it," said David, as if Tara was being perfectly reasonable. "Your hoop is safe with me."

David returned to the chair he had in the middle of the stack of hoops, like an eagle in a nest.

"Look," I said, after Tara had walked away. "Can I just have four hoops? Medium weight? Some of us need to practice. She won't see."

She was Mrs. Tyndall. The Royal She.

"She'll fire me," he said.

"So?" I said.

"So this is my job." He looked over at Kelli Ann.

"A made-up job," I said.

"A useful job," he said.

"Not as useful as walking Bao Bao," I said. "Which I would be willing to do on a day of your choosing if you can part with four Hula-Hoops for fifteen minutes."

David let out a breath. "Fine. But don't let her see you.

Do you know what the record is for spinning Hula-Hoops simultaneously?" He didn't wait for me to answer. "Sixty."

I took the Hula-Hoops to the end of the hall and turned the corner, where it dead-ended into a bunch of science classrooms. It was sort of like a hidden cul-de-sac. No one was watching.

"Ready?" I said to Duncan, Max, and Andy. "Go."

It was as if I'd said, "Throw the Hula-Hoop at the ground but hit a body part on the way down." On that count, they were successful.

"You move in a circle," I said.

Duncan turned around in a circle.

"You move your hips in a circle, you dope," I said. I took a hoop and put it around my waist. "When the hoop hits your left side, move your waist toward the left, and when it moves to the right, move your waist toward the right." It was weird to try to explain it. "You have to find your rhythm," I said.

Duncan lifted the hoop again.

We heard a swishing noise. Could a theater ghost leave the theater?

Swish. Swish. Swish.

"What are you kids doing here?"

It was not Mrs. Tyndall, but it was almost as bad. The school custodian, Mr. Shea, was standing there, holding a mop like a sword. And he was growling.

"Remedial Hula-Hooping?" I said. It was the truth.

Mr. Shea wasn't friendly like the elementary school custodians. He yelled at kids when they walked across his clean floors, and also when they didn't.

"Hand it over," growled Mr. Shea.

"Please," I said. "We'll go!"

"Hand it over," he said again.

I breathed out and handed him my hoop. The boys handed over their hoops, too, and we started to file by. David was going to kill me for losing four Hula-Hoops.

"Wait," Mr. Shea said. We froze.

Then Mr. Shea put all four hoops around his waist. He started rotating his hips and kept them all going at the same time.

"Whoa," Duncan said. "Mr. Shea, you should be in the play."

Mr. Shea stopped scowling and looked . . . pleased. I had never seen him look pleased about anything, but maybe it was hard to look pleased when you were cleaning up throw-up or getting balls off of the school roof. Now he looked like, well, a kid.

Finally he stopped swirling his hips. He stepped out of the hoops and handed them to us.

"Still got it," he said. "Don't leave any trash behind."

"Wait," I said. As the school custodian, Mr. Shea was all over Dwight D. Eisenhower Junior High. "Have you ever heard of a ghost in the auditorium?"

"Heh," said Mr. Shea. "I've worked at this school for eighteen years. It has some secrets."

I looked at the guys, who seemed more interested in the hoops. Mr. Shea's moves had been an inspiration. Duncan actually got the hoop to stay up for a few rotations, and Max no longer seemed to be actively working against the Hula-Hoop.

Someone coughed. We all looked up. But it was Tara.

"It's just Tara," I said. "No big deal."

"Actually," said Tara, "Mrs. Tyndall is looking for you guys, so it is kind of a big deal. The ensemble is supposed to stay in the auditorium."

"We'll be there in a minute," I said. "Mr. Shea said we could practice here. Hey, you should have seen Mr. Shea. He had four—"

"Mrs. Tyndall was really mad," Tara said.

"Mrs. Tyndall is always mad."

"Because you guys don't follow the rules," said Tara. "That's why we have a hoop wrangler now."

"We're here to practice for the show," I pointed out. "They're just getting the hang of it."

"You can't just run off and do what you feel like," said Tara.

For half a second, I hated Tara. And then I hated myself for hating her.

"C'mon," I said. Duncan picked up the Hula-Hoops,

and we walked back to the auditorium. Tara walked slightly ahead—near but not a part of us.

On Friday, I brought the hundred buttons to school with me. Mom had gotten mad because I'd stayed up late finishing them. My fingers were red and blue from the markers, and achy from making all the buttons. I'd also had to make sure I spelled BUCHANAN correctly every time after I realized I had made a BUCHACHAN button.

"Thanks," said Tara, taking the bag from me. "Mom said she'll give you the money the next time you come over."

I was wearing a new button that said PIMPLE SERFECTION, which I had made during a break from the Mrs. Buchanan buttons.

"What do you think?" I said, holding up the button. I wanted to make Tara laugh. I wanted to feel like we were on the same side again.

"I don't get it," said Tara.

"Mrs. Tyndall, remember? She was trying to say simple perfection?"

Tara tilted her head to one side. "Kind of?"

"Everyone laughed when she said it," I said, to make my point. Someone from the ensemble would have gotten it.

"Sorry," Tara said, pinning one of her mom's buttons to her jacket. She chose one that said BUCHANAN FOR MAYOR. I wondered if anyone would think she was running instead of her mom. "I must have missed it."

"Clearly."

"Don't be mad! I've been thinking about other stuff. I've got oratory on top of the play. County finals are tomorrow," said Tara. "Wish me luck! I'm going to wear the oratory button you made for me."

"Luck." I noticed that she didn't invite me, but honestly I was relieved that I didn't have to make up a reason not to go.

CHAPTER 20

THE TRUTH ABOUT PATSY

ON SATURDAY AFTERNOON, DAVID decided to go to Ear Wax to buy some music for Hector for his birthday. "You want to come with?" he said.

I nodded. "Hector's in character," I said. "He probably won't listen to anything that's popular now."

"Good point." David opened his world almanac and looked up bestselling songs from 1958.

"The number one song of 1958 was the first foreign-language song, 'Volare.' It means 'to fly.' But there are some Elvis songs on the charts."

"I think Elvis is safer," I said. "You're a not-terrible friend."

"You'd be surprised," said David. I wasn't sure if that meant he was better or worse than I expected.

On our way out, we found Wai Po in the family room

with Bao Bao and a box of biscuits. Bao Bao was looking very intently at Wai Po.

"I thought he was on a diet," said David.

I sang the jingle for Diet Coke but changed the words for Bao Bao. "Just for the joy of it . . . dog biscuit!"

"Always with the singing," Wai Po said. "Bao Bao is just as smart as that cat. I am teaching him commands in English and Chinese."

As far as I knew, Bao Bao did not follow commands in any language, so two seemed to be stretching it.

"Watch," said Wai Po. She turned to Bao Bao and held up a biscuit. "Bao Bao, zuo."

Bao Bao sat.

"Bao Bao, lai." She made a "come here" gesture with her hand.

Bao Bao looked confused. After a moment, he stretched his body out on the floor.

"He thinks she means lie down," David whispered to me.

"No! Bao Bao, lai," Wai Po repeated. Bao Bao rolled over onto his back and waited for a belly rub. David and I laughed.

Wai Po folded her arms and looked at Bao Bao. Bao Bao wagged his tail and then arched his back, still waiting. Wai Po reached down and scratched his tummy.

"You know," she said, "Bao Bao is very smart. He thinks for himself. Not just doing what everyone tells him to do."

While David was deciding on music for Hector, I went looking for Patsy Klein. Designer jeans were still my priority, but now that I knew I was getting money from Mrs. Buchanan, I figured I could splurge at Ear Wax, too. I had taped some of Patsy's songs off the radio, but they didn't sound as good as when Nashville Nick played them, especially since my tape captured the telephone ringing in the middle of "Crazy." Ear Wax sold new records and used ones, all mixed together in bins. They also sold tapes. Almost every bit of space was filled with music. Usually when I came here, I started by flipping through posters or the buttons by the cash register before looking at the albums. But this time, I was on a mission. I went through the *K*'s. Kajagoogoo. The Kinks. KISS.

No Patsy.

"Patsy Klein, I'm searching for you," I sang, in the achy way Patsy would have, which reminded me that I was looking in the rock section instead of country. Only I didn't find any Patsy Klein there, either.

The record clerk was reading a magazine and cranking the Ramones. She seemed to be trying to move as little as possible, except to move a French fry into her mouth from a greasy paper bag. She didn't even bop to the music. Maybe because she was afraid of knocking over the tapes that were stacked on the counter like the Leaning Tower of Pisa. She was the opposite of Nashville Nick, who was very enthusiastic about sharing his music preferences.

"Hey," I said. "Do you have any Patsy Klein?"

"Yes." She didn't look up.

I waited for her to say more, but she didn't. "Where would I find it?" I asked.

"Under Klein," she said.

"I looked through all of the *K*'s."

She put the magazine down on the counter in slow motion. "Try *C*," she said. She picked up the magazine again.

"*C*?"

She looked at me and saw my button. "Cline," she said. "*C-L-I-N-E*." She said this like I was the stupidest person she'd ever met.

I walked over to the *C*'s in a daze. It had never even occurred to me to spell her name with a *C*. *Klein* is Jewish. *Cline*, I was not so sure about.

Patsy Cline had a section all to herself. She had the most perfect skin you ever saw, and the reddest lipstick, the kind Safta never got on exactly right. Patsy must've been an expert at applying makeup. She was definitely not Chinese, but she wore her hair in a way I'd seen Wai Po's in an old photo. She also wore a cowboy shirt with fringes on it. Tara had a shirt like that for Halloween in second grade when she wanted to be a cowgirl; my parents said spending that kind of money on a costume was foolish.

I spent a long time looking at that album cover. Patsy Cline didn't look Jewish. But people said I didn't look Jewish, either. It was still inside me; it was still who I was. I went over and found the album among the cassettes. Records had better sound quality, but I couldn't play a record on my Walkman. This tape would be higher quality than what I was getting by putting my cassette recorder next to the radio. I thought about hiding my button before I went back to the counter, but the clerk had already seen it, so I decided to act like I'd spelled it that way on purpose. I went up to the counter and slapped the tape right on it. Clack.

She rang it up and didn't even tell me my total, just pointed to it on the cash register: $3.98.

"Only the good die young," said the clerk. It was a Billy Joel song, but she didn't look like the type of person who actually listened to Billy Joel.

I looked at her blankly. Who died young?

She pointed at the tape cover. At Patsy.

Patsy was dead?

My brain raced to keep up. Patsy was dead. That

wasn't right. Nashville Nick would have said something, wouldn't he?

My button business had been pretty steady, so I paid the clerk with some of my profits and waited for David. He had gone with an Elvis album that had old-fashioned lettering on the front. I thought back to the bin of Patsy Cline records. They looked old-fashioned, too. No recent covers. "If Hector sings nothing but Elvis for the next few weeks, this will be all your fault," I said, trying to think of something besides Patsy.

It didn't work. David pointed at the cassette in my hand. "Who is that?" I guessed he didn't hear what happened with the clerk.

"Patsy Cline."

"Was she the one you were listening to the other night?"

"Yup." David would probably know if she was Jewish. He would probably know if she was dead. But there was really only one person I wanted to ask.

That night, I waited until Nashville Nick played his first song before I called the station.

"WTRY. Nashville Nick at your musical service."

"Hi, Nash, it's Lauren. Lonesome L?"

"How's my favorite Patsy fan?"

I pulled on the phone cord and let it spring back. "I have a question," I said.

"You can ask me anything but my age and my salary. I'll just say one's too high and one's too low." He chuckled at his own joke.

"It's about Patsy." I had two questions, actually, but I wasn't sure which to ask first. "Was she Jewish?"

"Jewish?" He made a clicking sound; my dad did that when he was thinking sometimes. "No, ma'am, I don't believe so. She grew up singing in her church."

I had to hurry to get my second question out. "Patsy is still alive, though, right?"

Silence. Then, "I am so sorry." He waited a beat, and then added, "She died in a plane crash. Back in 1963."

1963. I started crying. At first I tried to cry quietly, so Nash wouldn't know, but then I had to take big gulps of air in between so I wouldn't suffocate.

"I should have realized," said Nash. For a moment, his voice lost its usual smoothness. "I'm sorry, I'm sorry. Of course you couldn't have known."

All my feelings swirled in my chest. The thing was, I still loved Patsy. I loved that when Patsy sang, I felt like someone knew exactly how I felt.

But when she was Jewish, we had even more of a connection. When she was a Jewish singer in country music, she gave me hope that I could go somewhere unexpected, a not-supposed-to.

But Patsy was dead before I was born. We didn't even overlap. I'd never get to meet her.

"I've got to go," I said.

"Wait—" said Nash. I didn't wait.

I hung up and stared at the phone. It looked the same. Same yellow cord. Same gray buttons. It seemed impossible that anything should still look the same after so much had changed.

I went outside and stood on my driveway in the dark. The stars were small, like someone had sprinkled the sky with glitter. I didn't know what to do with all the feelings inside me.

A year after Grandpa Joe died, we went to the unveiling of his headstone at the cemetery. We each picked up a rock and put it on the smooth gray granite. I wanted to honor Patsy the same way. I felt around in my driveway for a rock, but all I found were dark pieces of gravel, which didn't seem special enough. Then I found a stone that was smoother and rounder than the rest, like a river rock that had gotten in there by mistake. I picked it up and brought it inside. I wasn't sure where Patsy was buried, so I set my cassette tape on my windowsill and put the stone on top of it. There.

All this time I had been wondering about a ghost in the theater, and it had been Patsy who was no longer part of this earth. I stood there and mourned Patsy Klein, who was now Patsy Cline, and her beautiful voice that knew how I felt inside. I was mourning something else, too, that was harder to put into words. My connection to a dream.

CHAPTER 21

NO ONE WANTS A SAD EGG ROLL

ON TUESDAY, THE LEADS GOT THEIR
costumes. Tara got a blue dress that buttoned down the top
and flared out at the bottom. When she Hula-Hooped, the
dress swung like a bell. Mrs. Tyndall sighed.

"There she is!" Mrs. Tyndall said. "My all-American girl."

The day before, we found out on the announcements that
Tara had gotten second in county oratory. She said it was
okay, because the next phase, regionals, was the same weekend as our show. Still, I could tell that she was disappointed,
even if no one else could. Tara's way of dealing with disappointment, on those rare occasions when it happened, was
to act like everything was fine, and she was smiling extra hard.

She came over and twirled. "What do you think?" she
said. She had her hair up in a high ponytail, with a blue

ribbon that matched her dress. Her hair had been curled into beautiful, long spirals.

"Perfect," I said, feeling my throat getting tighter. She did look perfect, which made me feel more imperfect. Tara would always fit in, would always look like she deserved the starring role. In my mind, I still saw myself in the middle of the *Star Search* stage, in lead roles that weren't Bloody Mary. But what was the point? Would anyone else ever think I looked perfect in the spotlight?

I was not Mrs. Tyndall's all-American girl. Maybe I wasn't anybody's.

Hector skidded over to Tara. "Word to the bird. You are chrome plated! Love the hair!"

"When does the ensemble get their costumes?" asked Cheryl.

"It doesn't matter," I said. "We're supposed to blend in, not stand out like the leads. Maybe we should dress up as side dishes."

"I wish the ensemble cared as much about its sound as its looks," Mrs. Tyndall said. I thought I had kept my voice pretty low, but apparently not low enough. "Maybe the costumes will come quicker when you all sound better in 'The King Is Coming.'"

Mrs. Tyndall never thought we sounded good enough. First it was "Everything Is Still the Same." And now she was holding another song over our heads.

Maybe this was supposed to be the most I should hope for—a barely costumed ensemble member, out of the spotlight. A few weeks ago, I would have felt lucky to be in the ensemble. Anybody would have. But that was before Tara got the lead. That was when being in the ensemble felt like the beginning. Not the end.

The ensemble huddled in a circle. "Do that thing," said Duncan. "Do that thing where you tell us about what kind of person sings the song."

Everyone looked at me, waiting. I tried to dredge up something. "I don't know," I said. "Happy, I guess?"

"The King" was one of Elvis Presley's nicknames, and "The King Is Coming" was one of the ensemble's big numbers, where we all run around getting ourselves and the town ready for Elvis. The script said Elvis was supposed to come in on a motorcycle suspended on wires, though Mrs. Tyndall said that was not going to happen. And the motorcycle, apparently, was going to be made of cardboard.

The opening of the song is simple, a series of middle-C notes, sung slowly. A king-is-com-ing-to-our hum-ble town. We go up a note for the *hum* in *humble* and down a note in the word *town*.

I thought about Duncan's question. I knew exactly what kind of person would sing "The King Is Coming." Someone who was excited to meet the person they idolized. Who could think of nothing else until the moment happened and then would talk of nothing else afterward. The way I would have felt if I were going to meet Patsy. The way I had fantasized that someone would feel about meeting me one day.

Singing had always made me happy, but when I opened my mouth to sing this time, sadness poured into me, drowning me. My lungs tightened, struggling for air. My eyes watered. It was all a tease, a cruel joke. I wasn't going to be a star.

I shut my eyes, willing myself not to cry. *Don't cry. Don't cry.*

If I cried, the ensemble wouldn't know what to do. We wouldn't get our costumes. Mrs. Tyndall would win again. If I started crying, I might never stop.

Then a voice in my head said, "Don't sing."

So I didn't.

Somehow I made it through the rest of practice, faking my way through the songs, the right mouth shapes and expressions. I opened my mouth in a round O when we sang, *Here comes that singing dynamo, born and raised in Tupelo!* I made an excited face when we pointed and sang with increasing volume, *I can see him! I can see him! I CAN SEE HIM!*

I was wondering if anyone would notice that I wasn't singing, when Mrs. Tyndall called me over. "I'd like a moment to speak to you," she said.

I dropped my head and walked over to her. Tara and I

normally walked home together, but she was walking out with Hector and Jennifer. She waved.

I motioned for her to come with me. If Tara was with me, then Mrs. Tyndall couldn't, or maybe wouldn't, yell at me. But Tara wasn't looking in my direction anymore.

Great. I turned to face Mrs. Tyndall, bracing myself for another scolding. But she smiled.

Smiled?

"I want you to know, Lauren, that I know you've been trying to be a better member of the ensemble. Especially after the Hula-Hoop incident. I see how the other members look up to you, and that you are acting like the leader I knew you could be," she said. "In light of that, I would like to offer you a small solo in the Elvis number."

She meant the part of the song where different people sing about what they're doing to make the town better for Elvis. There was a line for a girl to sing: *I'm washing the windows till they gleam! In the cutest town he's ever seen!* Right now, we were singing it all together, but Mrs. Tyndall was making it a solo.

And offering it to me.

And not even noticing that I didn't sing.

"Um," I said. Maybe my singing didn't even matter.

Mrs. Tyndall looked at me with a mixture of curiosity and irritation. It must have felt like seeing Bao Bao not getting excited over a treat.

"I think you should give the solo to Hallelujah," I said finally. "Or Cheryl."

"That's not your decision," said Mrs. Tyndall. "You're really not taking it? Don't expect me to offer it again."

"I understand," I said. And nothing more.

The rain makes me think of all sorts of songs. "Raindrops Keep Fallin' on My Head." "Singin' in the Rain." "A Hard Rain's A-Gonna Fall." But when I woke up the next morning to a cool spring rain, the songs weren't coming out of me. I could think of them, the way I thought about math problems, but they weren't bubbling up inside me anymore. Wherever they had been before was a dead space.

I went down to the kitchen to have breakfast. When I said good morning, Wai Po jumped about a foot in the air.

"Ai ya! You scared me. Don't sneak up on me like that."

"I didn't sneak up on you."

"I usually hear you coming down the hallway because you are singing this thing or that thing. You are never quiet. Sneaking!"

I didn't argue with her. I poured myself a bowl of cereal and listened to the sound of crunching in my head. David walked in and stopped. "Oh, you're here."

"You're a genius."

"No, it's just that I usually hear you when you get up."

"That's what I said," Wai Po chimed in. "Singing."

"How am I supposed to know the weather if you're not singing about rain or sun or whatever."

"Duh. Look out the window." I hated when David was like that, all smug and know-it-all. It was worse when he was right.

"Oh, come on," said David. "One little tune. What about 'Itsy-Bitsy Spider'?" He started making the finger motions.

"Sing it yourself," I said.

I faked my way through another practice that afternoon. In some ways it was easier, because we were rehearsing another song that starred Tara, "All-American Town," so I just had to stand in the background and be part of the chorus. But in another way, it was worse.

> My town's an all-American town,
> We all say "how do you do?"
> When the day starts anew.

Tara skipped around the stage, waving to the audience and then waving to the people who represented the town. We were all supposed to smile adoringly at her and wave back.

> My town's an all-American town,
> Where we have no division.
> We watch the same news on the television.

My town's an All-American town,
We root for our baseball team
And then go out for ice cream.

Tara pantomimed cheering at a baseball game and we followed along, pretending to watch a home run.

My town's an All-American town,
Where I found inspiration
In a new innovation.

Then the ensemble joined in, with Tara still clearly in the front. The star, the special one, against the backdrop of the rest of us.

What took us so long?
How could we be so wrong?
You can see our hips shakin',
And there's just no mistakin' . . .

Then Tara got in one more line: *THIS IS MY AMERICAN TOWN!!!*

Mrs. Tyndall clapped at the end, which she rarely did. "That's more like it!" she said. Then she added, "Tara, you really set off the ensemble quite well." For a moment, I was glad I hadn't been singing. I didn't want any part of Mrs. Tyndall's praise.

Tara grabbed my arm as we filed offstage and Hector walked on. "What is going on? Why do you look like that?"

She peered into my face. She had this way of looking at me that made me feel that I couldn't keep secrets from her. It was the same expression when she got me to confess that I liked Luke Bendach last year.

"Maybe because Mrs. Tyndall acts like the ensemble has no value on its own. It's all about the leads," I said, mentally emphasizing the word *maybe*.

"It's not like that."

"Who got a special Hula-Hoop? Who already has a costume? And solos?" I asked. It felt good to take a break from feeling sad, even if it was by feeling mad instead.

Tara shook her head. From her expression, she wasn't too happy, either.

Cheryl came by. "What's going on with you two?"

"Nothing," the not-very-Royal We said at the same time.

Cheryl tugged at my arm. "Come on, Lauren. We're going to rehearse out in the hall."

"How did you pull that off?" I asked. "Mrs. Tyndall never allows us that far from her clutches."

"We begged Mr. Shea," said Cheryl. Mr. Shea had been stopping by to watch the rehearsals, so it was only a matter of time before Mrs. Tyndall looped him in.

We had the whole hallway to ourselves, so we spread out and worked on matching the singing to the movement. The singing was okay. The hooping was not. Part of the problem was we were all trying to move the Hula-Hoops to the music, but if we couldn't hoop fast enough, the song, "In the Middle of the Circle," lagged.

"You're spinning too fast," Hallelujah said.

"You're starting too late," said Andy.

"You're singing to the speed of the Hula-Hoop, but it should be the other way around."

"We're never going to get our costumes."

We stopped practicing completely and kept arguing.

Mr. Shea tapped his mop on the floor, and we stopped.

"Mm," he said.

"You got any ideas?" I asked him.

He shook his head. "Be happy with mediocrity."

"That's it!" said David, who had been sent into the hall as our second babysitter.

"Mediocrity?" I said. I did not think that word was in Mrs. Tyndall's vocabulary.

"Being happy," he said. "That's the point of the song, right? That's the whole point of the Hula-Hoop: It's for everyone. If you mess it up, it's still fun. As long as everyone looks like they're having a good time, the scene will work. The audience will think you're messing up on purpose."

"I don't mess up," Hallelujah said.

"You don't have to," David said. "That's the point, too. Hula-Hooping is for people of all levels."

I thought about Mr. Shea's face when he was showing us

how to Hula-Hoop—that expression of delight that made him look like a kid.

The hoop wrangler was right.

"Okay," I said. "Let's relax and not worry about being perfect. Mr. Shea, will you count us off?"

Mr. Shea tapped his mop on the floor. And we started. I didn't sing, but I did everything else. The movements, the expressions. And I watched. We were better in a weird way, but maybe only because we had started looking at the number differently.

> *C'mon and join us for some Hula-Hoop glee,*
> *Where the hoop spins round and your heart goes whee!*
> *Don't you wish you could always feel this free?*
> *In the middle of the circle that goes round.*

Hallelujah added one of the more difficult moves, where she caught the hoop mid-spin and lifted it over her head while keeping the hoop spinning. Andy actually managed a few spins before the hoop dropped. Duncan and Cheryl were hooping in sync. And everyone was smiling.

Mr. Shea nodded, even though we weren't up to his speed.

We stopped trying to be exactly like one another while still trying to be together. *Ensemble.*

That night Wai Po had a big announcement. "I got you a job! Like the T-shirt store, only better," she said.

It was a gig at her friend's Chinese restaurant. They wanted me to dress up like an egg roll and sing to attract the lunch crowd.

"But a happy egg roll," she said, looking at my face. "No one wants a sad egg roll."

I shook my head. "I don't think I can."

Wai Po frowned but didn't say anything.

The next day after Hebrew school, Safta came over with her own announcement.

"Remember the man from the shoe store? He's having a sale and he wants you to sing."

I knew tons of songs about shoes. "These Boots Are Made for Walkin'." "Blue Suede Shoes." "Goody Two Shoes." But instead of feeling like a person singing about their new shoes, I felt like the gum stuck to the sole.

"I can't," I told Safta.

"Why not? It's an opportunity." Wai Po nodded. For once they were on the same side.

"I have to save my voice for the play," I lied.

But the truth was, I didn't have to save my voice for anything at all.

CHAPTER 22

FEELING MAD AT MRS. TYNDALL/ "IT'S NOT MY FAULT"

MRS. TYNDALL STOPPED US HALFWAY through "The King Is Coming." "Girls, why aren't you singing louder? Someone's grandmother needs to hear you from the back row."

The thing was, the girls were singing pretty loudly, even without me. But Tara, Hector, Ricky, and the rest of the main characters were standing around talking. Hector let out one of his weird reverse-snorts. Who could hear over that?

The sets were now coming into place. For this song, the stage was divided up into four scenes, to represent places around the town. There was a toy store, a classroom, the inside of the Goresons' kitchen, and a post office. The kitchen had been set up to look like they were about to have dinner.

Someone had even found a glass bottle of milk, like they had had in the 1950s.

Mrs. Tyndall made us start from the top. Lila had been given the solo Mrs. Tyndall had offered to me, but she had barely started when Mrs. Tyndall stopped the song. "No! No! No! You have to be louder! And on key!"

Lila was not used to getting yelled at by Mrs. Tyndall. From the corner of my eye, I could see her eyes filling with tears, but she was trying not to cry. Maybe if I had taken the solo, Lila wouldn't be getting screamed at.

Ricky leaned in to whisper something to Tara, and in that moment of silence, Tara burst out laughing.

We should all try to be more considerate

And by we I mean... YOU!

Maybe I was letting down the ensemble in some ways, but I was still going to defend us. Side dishes stuck together. I raised my hand. "Mrs. Tyndall, part of the problem is that it's kind of noisy in here." I looked over at Tara and company to make my point clear.

Duncan chimed in. "Yeah, when they practice, we have to sit and be quiet. It's not fair that they get to stand around and talk."

Mrs. Tyndall motioned for the group to sit down, which they did, slowly. "I'm trying to let them build rapport," she said, as if it was our fault that we were bothered by their talking. "I need that chemistry to come through to the audience. They're the ones carrying the story."

Mrs. Tyndall had just finished saying the word *story* when a long, low whistling sound began. The cap on the milk suddenly flew up, and the bottle began spraying hot, sour milk all over the ensemble.

Mrs. Tyndall began screaming at us to stay calm, but no one stays calm with a face full of sour milk. We ran offstage, gagging.

"Don't run!" screamed Mrs. Tyndall. "You'll slip!"

"It's the ghost!" yelled Duncan. The white droplets of milk stuck to his hair, his skin. The whole ensemble was spattered in white.

"The ghost is mad at Mrs. Tyndall," I said to Lila as we ran-walked toward the bathroom. "For being unfair to the ensemble."

Mrs. Tyndall did not get the memo about the ghost being mad at her. Instead, after we had all washed off, she made the ensemble come back and clean off the stage with rags and Lysol.

"It's not our fault," said Hallelujah.

"It happened while you were onstage," snapped Mrs. Tyndall.

"The prop master should have checked the bottle," said Andy. Apparently sour milk erased Russian accents.

Tina, the prop master, surveyed the damage. "I don't know where that bottle came from."

"The theater ghost brought it," whispered Duncan.

"That was real milk, getting hotter and hotter under the lights," said Andy.

"Or someone in the ensemble decided to play a little prank," said Mrs. Tyndall. Which made no sense, because if we were going to spray sour milk on someone, it wouldn't be ourselves. Of course, Mrs. Tyndall never thought it could have been one of the leads.

I thought Tara might talk the rest of the leads into coming up to help. But instead, she just sat in her seat and watched us work.

"Thanks for all your help," I said as we walked home.

Tara looked at me, wide-eyed. "Mrs. Tyndall said the ensemble should do it."

"She didn't say the leads couldn't do it," I said.

We walked a little longer in silence. I shouldn't be mad, I told myself. Maybe Tara was right. It's not like she told them to help.

I took the headphones from my Walkman and slipped them over her ears. "Hey. Listen to this song." I pushed PLAY on "Crazy." It was getting a little easier to listen to Patsy again. Her voice still calmed me down.

Tara listened. "Is this . . . country music?" She wrinkled her nose like she could still smell the milk.

I stopped the tape player. "That's not what I meant to play," I said. "It must have been something David recorded. Brothers."

"Weird," Tara said.

"It's just different from what we listen to," I said. I was defending Patsy more than anything. More than myself.

"You should keep an eye on David," she said.

"Or an ear," I said.

Tara laughed. Everything was so easy for her. She liked what everybody was supposed to like. She looked like what the lead was supposed to look like. She wore what everyone was supposed to wear. I pulled my shirt down over the Sylvia Soupson label of my jeans.

"You look so bummed out when you're onstage," Tara said.

"You would, too, if Mrs. Tyndall yelled at you all the time instead of telling you that you look perfect." I tried to sound like I was joking by drawing out the word *per-fect*.

"Are you mad that I got cast as Brenda Sue?" asked Tara.

I thought about her question. Mad didn't seem like quite the right word. It just seemed like those things my mom and grandmothers always said—*you can be anything!*—were for people like Tara.

What would a Sweet and Supportive friend say? "No." What would a Tough but True friend add? "Not exactly?"

Apparently my non-answer was an answer for Tara. "You can't be mad at me," said Tara. Her voice was part demanding, part pleading. "I didn't do anything wrong. I even made you check with Mrs. Tyndall."

"You're right," I said. I swallowed hard. "I'm not mad." But it was like cleaning up after the bottle of milk—maybe just following the rules wasn't enough.

Tara looped her arm through mine. "I wouldn't be able to stand it if you were mad at me."

Before I could think of what to say next, a car slowed down next to us. It was Dad in the station wagon. He'd just gotten off a shift at the hospital. Tara and I looked at each other and made a silent agreement not to argue in front of him.

"Hi, Mr. Horowitz," said Tara cheerfully. "Thanks for the surprise ride." She opened the back door and slid in. I got in the opposite side, behind Dad.

"How was rehears— What's that smell?!"

"There was an incident with a bottle of milk and a cranky teacher," I said. "The ensemble had to clean the whole set."

Tara didn't say anything.

"Well, roll down the windows. I know what will cheer you up." Dad slid a cassette into the tape player. It was *Goodbye*

Yellow Brick Road by Elton John. One of my all-time favorite albums to sing along to. The opening piano notes of the title track filled the car. Dad said he knew I could sing the first time he heard me singing along when I was little.

Tara started to sing along, but I leaned over the seat and hit the power button to turn it off.

Dad and Tara looked at me, mouths open.

"I think quiet is nice sometimes, don't you?" I said. I spent the rest of the car ride home looking out the window.

That night, before dinner, I took a shower and got out one of my photo albums. I had three of them, one from when I was a baby, one from preschool to third grade, and one from fourth grade to now. The third one was almost full.

I looked at my school pictures, the ones from when I was missing a tooth, and the one from when I decided to give myself bangs. There were some of me and Tara, too. Dancing, a blurred three-legged race together from field day last year.

My mom came in and sat next to me. "What are you doing?"

"Nothing." Wishing it were last year. Wishing things were back to the way they used to be. Wishing I looked like everyone else.

Mom pointed to last year's class photo. "There you are. I can always spot you right away."

"Because I'm the only Chinese kid in my class."

"Because you're my daughter, and I know you from the way you stand, the way you smile, the way you do everything." She gave me a squeeze.

It's because I'm the only one with black hair, I thought. But that gave me an idea. "Can I color my hair?" If I couldn't support the ensemble with my voice, maybe it would help if I looked more like the other kids.

"Why on earth would you want to do that?"

"For the show," I said. I tried to say it in a way that kind of sounded like Mrs. Tyndall was asking for it. "It's so I can blend with the rest of the ensemble." I heard my voice catch and stopped talking. Why did I always have to look like me?

"What color would you make it?"

"Maybe light brown?"

"I don't think those chemicals are good for you."

"Wai Po uses chemicals to perm her hair," I pointed out.

"That's different," said Mom. "You are still young. No one your age colors their hair." She reached over and touched my hair. "Your hair is beautiful just the way it is," she said. "Don't do anything to it."

I used to love it when Mom played with my hair, but now I pulled away from her. "You have to say that. You're my mom."

Wai Po stopped by my room. "Dinner will be ready soon."

Mom sighed. "Oh good."

"I made ning meng ji," said Wai Po. That made me feel a little better. David and I both loved lemon chicken, the way

Wai Po made it, not the fried restaurant kind. "No fighting over it. I made a double batch."

I wasn't done making my case, though. "Can I color my hair if I don't use chemicals?" I asked Mom.

Mom sighed. "I really don't think it's possible."

"But if it is, can I?" I asked

David called for Mom. The phone rang. "Dinner in ten minutes?" asked Wai Po.

"Can I?" I asked.

Mom threw her hands up in the air. "What? Oh my goodness. Yes. Yes!"

Technically I wasn't sure if Mom was saying yes to Wai Po, David, or me. But it was close enough, wasn't it?

The next day, on the way home from school, I stopped at Holmes's and bought a bottle of Sun In. Some of the older girls at my pool sprayed Sun In onto their hair to make blonde highlights, like lemon juice but faster. I wasn't expecting that, but I figured I would probably get something. Probably like a nice light brown.

Right before bed, I stood in the bathroom and brushed my always-black, always-straight hair.

David stopped by and watched me. "Are you using the bathroom?"

"Does it look like I'm using the bathroom?"

"When I say using the bathroom, I mean the toilet, specifically," he said.

"I think you can tell I'm not using the toilet."

"What ARE you doing?"

"I'm trying to figure out what to do with my hair for the show. Make it look different." I held up the bottle of Sun In.

"Are you sure that's okay with Mom and Dad?"

"Mom said not to use chemicals," I said. "This is more natural. It's basically just lemon juice. And I'm going to braid it so it's wavy, too."

"Like when you and Tara played *Little House on the Prairie*?"

"Yeah, like that." I was surprised David remembered something like that. Now I had a huge favor to ask. "Will you do the Sun In part? I don't want to do too much, but I also don't want to have any blotchy patches in the back or anything."

"I guess that makes me a . . . hair wrangler?" said David.

"It makes you a not-terrible brother," I said.

David sprayed my hair, making sure to go from the top to the bottom.

"Not too much," I reminded him. The bathroom was already smelling very lemony.

"Yeah, yeah. Girls are so weird," said David. "I'm planning to have this haircut with this hair color until I'm eighty." Then, because he was David, he added, "Did you know that in ancient Greece, a ruler sent a secret message to a friend by shaving a slave's head and tattooing a message on his scalp? By the time he reached enemy territory, his hair had grown over the message."

"So then he had to get his head shaved again when he reached the friend?"

"Yup."

I started braiding my hair. "I'm not planning on being anyone's secret messenger."

David watched me finish the second braid. "You missed a lot of hair."

"I'm making smaller braids to get a tighter wave," I said. "And then I'm going to blow-dry the braids because I think you need heat to activate the Sun In."

He studied my head. "By my calculations, you're going to need about six more braids to get all your hair."

"You're going to need to be about six times less weird to join normal society," I said.

"Normal is overrated," said David.

Maybe normal was overrated. But for the first time in my life, I was going to look like everyone else and I couldn't wait.

CHAPTER 23

WHAT'S WRONG WITH TIGERS?

THAT NIGHT, I DREAMED I WAS IN A book of fairy tales, and all the princesses wanted my hair. Patsy's song "Sweet Dreams" drifted around us, achy and lovely. Rapunzel cried because her hair was too light, and dark hair was better. Also, she wanted trout. Sleeping Beauty woke up for me, not the prince, and her first question was how to get waves like mine. Snow White tugged on her hair, and it magically became longer, just like the Crissy doll I still had tucked away in the basement. In the dream, I didn't talk, I just smiled and danced into the next story.

It was one of those dreams that is so involved you don't hear the alarm go off and you have to be woken up by your brother pounding on the door. "Hey, Little House, you're going to be late for school!"

I jumped out of bed and ran to the bathroom. To save

time, I started taking out the ponytail holders while I used the toilet. Then I ran my fingers through my braids to undo them, shook out my hair, and jumped in front of the mirror to see the full effect.

Oh no!

I had imagined long, flowy, light brown curls. Instead, I had orange stripes in my hair. My very, very voluminous wavy hair.

I may have screamed.

David came running. "What's the matter?"

I pointed to my hair. "This is the matter! You made me look like a tiger! A stripy, stupid tiger!"

"You said not to do too much!"

"So?"

"So I did half your hair, as measured out in regular intervals. And what's wrong with tigers?"

"I don't want to look like a tiger! I meant lightly, all over!"

"I was just trying to be mathematical about it." David gave me a long look. "I think you look kind of cool. Like Van Halen. I gotta go. I can't be late."

I looked at the clock. I had about two minutes before I would have to run the entire way to school.

I started the tap and started pressing handfuls of water on my hair. Go down, go down. Be less orange, be less orange. It didn't do either. Now I had springy *and* wet striped hair. I looked around the bathroom for help. I pumped a dollop of coconut-scented moisturizer onto my hair, which made it springy, wet, and, because my hair already had a lemon scent, smelling like a tropical fruit salad.

Wai Po came upstairs. "Eh? Why haven't you left for school? You should have left already!"

"I can't go to school." I pointed to my head.

"If you are not sick, you go to school," she said. "Hair is not important." Then she said, "It's orange. Does your mother know your hair is orange?"

"If I go to school like this," I said, "I will die from embarrassment."

"Put on a hat," said Wai Po. "You do not want a tardy!" Making sure David and I left for school on time was one of Wai Po's jobs, and she took it very seriously. She seemed to think a tardy went on her permanent record, not mine.

I didn't have any hats, but David did, from the one time he played Little League. I ran into his room, grabbed his baseball cap, and pulled my hair through the hole in the back. A baseball cap would have the bonus of making me look more all-American. Maybe I could find a hot dog and run around with that, too. *What about now, Mrs. Tyndall? Who's your all-American girl now?*

Wai Po looked at me. "Your hair is as big as your head. And you look like a lao hu."

Of course, David had played for the Tigers, so the hat and my hair looked like some terrible costume. My hair came out in a large poof in the back. Then the hat sprang backward. The waves on top of my head had popped it off, like popcorn pushing the lid off a pot.

I ripped the hat off and let out a scream, which was the loudest I'd been since I stopped singing. Wai Po covered her ears and shouted, "IT'S NOT THAT BAD."

"It is," I said. I pushed down on my hair for what seemed like the millionth time and watched it spring back up. I wondered if there was something that could reverse Sun In. Sun Out? "Please can I stay home?"

"No," said Wai Po. "You are not missing school for this. When I was your age, we were only allowed to have hair down to here." She pointed to a spot about half an inch below her earlobe. "Maybe that was a good idea. Stop worrying about looks and focus on books." She smiled at her rhyme.

I grabbed a bandana, folded it into a triangle, and tied it around my head. The cloth billowed out slightly, but it was the best look I had so far. I grabbed my backpack and ran out of the house. I thought about skipping school, but they called home when you did that. I wished I could beam myself into homeroom instead of wading through the hallway. I wished I could beam myself into outer space. I'll bet everybody had bad hair in zero gravity.

CHAPTER 24

SIDE DISHES STICK TOGETHER

I HOPED I COULD GO A FEW PERIODS before anyone recognized me. But Cheryl recognized me about ten seconds after I walked through the door.

"Lauren!" She grabbed me by the arm and pulled me behind one of the pillars in the hallway. "What happened?"

"It's a long story."

She took a step back and studied me. "I assume this is not your preferred hairstyle."

I shook my head and peeked around the pillar. The hallway was still filled with kids.

"I want to go home."

"No, look, everything's going to be fine," said Cheryl. "We just have to be creative." She reached into her backpack and pulled out a banana clip. Banana clips were the latest thing for hair; they looked like two wide-toothed combs joined at one end on a hinge.

She bent over and spun her hair around the comb. When she stood back up, her hair was in a bun.

"How did you . . . ?"

"Grab your backpack." We started down the hall, and Cheryl stopped at the first person who stared at me.

"Hi! We're with the musical, and we're trying out new hairstyles. Can you give us some feedback?" said Cheryl. She turned and modeled her bun, and then motioned for me to do the same. I forced myself to smile.

"Uhhhh. I like your hairstyle? I guess?"

"Duly noted." Cheryl pulled a notebook from her backpack and made a mark in it. "That's one for the updo. Thanks for your input!"

We made our way down the hallway like that, Cheryl carrying out her fake survey, and me pretending that this was intentional. Shockingly some kids picked my hairdo.

"It's different," said one girl. "The other one is kind of boring."

Then the first-period bell rang. I grabbed Cheryl's arm. "What am I going to do now? I can't do this without you." Giving up Cheryl felt like giving up a shield in the middle of a battle.

"Just keep doing what we've been doing. It's for the play; it was totally intentional," said Cheryl. "Just make it through first period."

"Thanks," I said. "You're totally saving me."

I made it through history, in part because Mr. Harper is one of those awesome teachers who likes to do funny stuff with students. In this case, I thought it was especially nice of him because Mr. Harper was bald.

"Who thinks this is a good hairstyle for the play? And not a good hairstyle?" Mr. Harper looked over the class. "Looks like the class would prefer a different hairstyle." I smiled and pretended to make a mark in my notebook. "Sometimes you want a more dramatic look, or you're trying to convey a certain characteristic."

"Like bald teacher," said Tony.

"That's from the stress of teaching you guys," said Mr. Harper. He ran his hand over his head. "Before I started teaching, I had a head full of thick, beautiful hair." He looked at me. "I never styled it quite like that, though."

―――――――――――――――――

Second period was Home Ec with Mrs. Shrewsbury, who was not as nice as Mr. Harper. She said she had to be strict because kids could get hurt on the stove or the sewing machines if they didn't follow directions. We were scheduled to start learning about sewing machines that day.

I held my breath and walked into the sewing room. Then I heard, "Psst. Lauren!"

I looked over and saw Hallelujah, patting the sewing machine next to her. She had straightened her bangs in the front, and then pulled the rest of her hair into a ponytail and added a headband. She looked very 1950s.

I ran over and squeezed next to her. "I can't believe it."

Mrs. Shrewsbury walked over and stared at us. "What, exactly, is going on here?" she asked.

"We're testing out hairstyles for the play," said Hallelujah.

"I don't know anything about hairstyles for the play, but I do know that these are very safe hairstyles." She raised her voice to address the class. "Class! I'd like to point out these very safe hairstyles that Lauren and Hallelujah are wearing. Lauren's kerchief is keeping her hair away from the sewing machine, and so is Hallelujah's ponytail and headband."

The rest of the class turned and stared at us blankly. Just like that, Mrs. Shrewsbury had made my hair seem like the most boring thing in the world.

"Maybe we should all make kerchiefs as a project," said Mrs. Shrewsbury. "But first, let's learn the parts of the sewing machine."

"So what's really going on?" whispered Hallelujah.

"I wanted to look . . ." I almost said *like everyone else*, but then realized how stupid that sounded. Hallelujah was the only black girl in the musical. I hadn't even thought about that. "I wanted to look different," I said. Different from me. The same as everybody else.

"No, I get it," said Hallelujah. "I get it." She let out a long breath. "Like take a break, right?"

"Yeah," I said. I pointed at my hair. "You see how well that turned out."

"People see what they want to see. There are four other black girls in this school. We look nothing alike but I get called by their names all the time."

"That stinks," I said. I wasn't sure what was worse: being confused for other people, or being the only person.

"What did your mom say?"

"She hasn't seen it yet."

"Is she going to kill you?"

"Probably. Technically I didn't break her rules, but my mom wants to go to law school. She'll find a way to make me guilty."

Hallelujah looked at my orange stripes. "Or she might decide you've been punished enough," she said.

I held my breath as I walked into science. So far, everyone who had helped me out was in the ensemble. Would Tara help me? If she didn't, everyone would find out that we weren't really doing a hairstyle test.

Tara's eyes widened when she saw my hair. "That's . . . electric."

"We're telling everyone that we're testing hairstyles for the musical." I grinned wildly.

Chris Pohansky came over. "Why isn't your hair different?" he asked Tara.

What I wanted was for Tara to pull her hair into a high ponytail, smile at Chris, and play along. She could do a fifties look in thirty seconds. But instead, she shrugged and said, "It's an ensemble thing, I guess."

Chris walked away. I stood, staring openmouthed at Tara.

"What?" said Tara. "What's wrong?"

I couldn't believe Tara didn't know what was going on. Couldn't she see? "Nothing," I said. Like the connection between us. Nothing.

Aside from Tara, the rest of the day went to plan. Duncan slicked back his hair like Hector. It was a style called a ducktail because it made a tiny flip at the base of his neck. Lila coaxed her hair into big, glamorous rolls. By the time we made it to rehearsal, the entire school had an opinion about our hairstyles, and no one thought I was out of the ordinary, except for the orange part.

Mrs. Tyndall came over to our section and shook her head slowly. "I've been hearing some pretty strange rumors about you all day today."

We looked at her innocently. "Good publicity for the play, huh?" asked Duncan.

"I hope you sound better than you look," she said.

After she walked away, I whispered, "Thanks, guys."

"Side dishes stick together," said Cheryl.

When we had a break, I went out to the bathroom to look at my hair. My stupid, striped hair. It had lost a little bit of volume during the day, but you could still see the stripes. A good shampoo and conditioner might fix the volume. But it wouldn't fix the color.

Maybe there wasn't a ghost in the theater. Maybe there was just a curse.

CHAPTER 25

MY GRANDMOTHER'S DAUGHTER

AS I HAD GUESSED, MY MOM DIS-
covered a loophole and found me guilty of Using Chemicals
to Color My Hair because even though it was mostly natural, Sun In had extra ingredients. I think she was really mad
about my hair. She kept looking over at me, sighing and
shaking her head. Because we had Saturday rehearsal, I was
really only grounded for a day and a half. At least I had an
excuse not to leave the house with my tiger hair.

My grandmothers tried to make my grounding less terrible by bringing things to me. Wai Po went to the library and
brought home a stack of books. Safta brought a black handbag with a mesh screen when she came over Sunday night to
watch TV with us. A little kitty face was poking out.

"Mini!" I scooped her up and gave her a little kiss.

"I thought the expression was 'cat out of the bag,' not 'cat in the bag,'" said Wai Po.

"It's no different than having a dog on a leash," Safta said. Then she added, "Except Beatrice Minerva is tidier. Remember: She can use the toilet."

Wai Po lifted Bao Bao onto her lap. He started licking the newspaper. She put him down, and he started following Mini, sniffing. Mini ignored him.

"Beatrice Minerva has another new trick," announced Safta. She cleared her throat. "Beatrice Minerva, I would like to watch some TV. TV, Minerva."

Mini, who had not yet learned that cats sometimes hiss when there's a dog in the room, walked over to the TV and looked at the screen for a minute.

"It's not even on," said Wai Po. She seemed pleased.

But then Mini got up on her hind legs and stretched her small body into a long one. She tapped the power button on the TV with her paw, one, two, three times. The TV screen came to life.

My parents clapped while Safta gave Mini a treat. "That's really something," said Dad.

"Can you teach her how to change channels?" asked David.

"If you get a new TV with a remote," said Safta.

"We won't be buying a new anything until after Lauren's bat mitzvah," said Mom. I noticed she did not mention law school, which was also expensive. I knew because she had a fat catalog of law schools that she kept on the coffee table.

Safta looked at Wai Po. "It's so nice to have a helpful companion."

Wai Po ignored Safta's dig. "It's almost *Star Search* time!"

"We can watch something else," I said.

My parents gave each other a look. "You love *Star Search*," said Mom.

"I did. Now I don't," I said.

"But this is the other thing I wanted to show you," said Safta. "I am making you a Nudie suit." She pulled out a piece of bright red cloth.

It was a red button-down, western shirt with two pockets in the front. The arms were trimmed with fringe, and a sparkly flower had started to make its way up one side.

"For when you are a star," said Safta proudly.

"Or if you are ever stranded on a remote island," said Wai Po. "And need to be seen from the air."

"I thought you like red," said Safta.

"I like red," said Wai Po. "This is very shiny."

"That's beautiful," said Mom. "You like it, don't you, Lauren?" She used that voice that parents use when you're supposed to play along. "It would be perfect for *Star Search*."

"I just said I don't like *Star Search*," I said. "But I suppose I should get used to that."

"Get used to what?" asked Mom.

"You not knowing stuff about me," I said. "When you go to law school. You'll be paying attention to that, not me." I expected Mom to get mad and maybe we would have a fight about her going to law school. Instead she folded her hands in her lap and studied them.

"We seem to have gotten a long way from why you aren't watching *Star Search*, which has nothing to do with law school," she said.

"You already sound like a lawyer," I said. But I didn't say it like a compliment.

"And you sound like those kids on *Star Search*," said Safta. Who did say it like a compliment. She folded up the shirt carefully and put it back in her purse.

"I can't even get a good part in the school play," I said.

"Oh, Lauren," said Mom. "Just because you didn't get the lead one time, you can't be so quick to give up."

"It's not one time," I said. "It's the way it is."

"It's because the director said that Lauren doesn't look American," said David.

Mom walked over and turned off the TV without any help from Mini. "What did you say?"

"Everyone said Lauren had the best audition and should have gotten a main role." I had forgotten he'd been there, too. "But she didn't get the part because she didn't look all-American. Like Tara."

"According to?" said Mom.

"Mrs. Tyndall," I said. "I told you I was in the ensemble."

"But that other part I had not heard," said Mom.

"Because you were away for work."

"Lauren," said Dad sharply. "I was here, and you could

have told me. And we were excited that you made the ensemble."

Mom tapped her fingertips together. "Making the ensemble *is* an achievement, but I want to know more about Mrs. Tyndall," she said.

"She wanted the audience to have a good experience," I said as I walked out of the room. "I wasn't her all-American girl."

Right before bed, Wai Po knocked on my door. "I want to talk to you," she said. She walked in and sat at my desk.

I nodded. I was actually surprised that I hadn't gotten in trouble for talking to Mom the way I did. Instead, I had been up in my room, trying to think of new buttons to make. DISAPPOINTMENT came to mind. EMBRACE MEDIOCRITY. WHY DREAM?

Wai Po sighed. "My daughter is sad, because her daughter is sad."

It took me a second to realize that *her daughter* meant me. It took me another moment to realize that Wai Po probably thought of Mom the same way that Mom thought of me.

"So why won't your daughter come talk to her daughter?" I asked.

"She thinks you are mad about law school," Wai Po said.

"That's true," I said.

"And that you need some time," she said.

I nodded. When she didn't say anything else, I felt obligated to fill the silence.

"I've just decided that singing is not for me," I said. "You should like that. You never liked me singing for other people anyway."

"That's not true!" said Wai Po. "I was worried that when you perform for strangers, people might think you are not a nice girl."

"Like, I am a mean person?"

"No, no. Like you are not a respectable girl. That you are from a not-good family," she said. "Performing for people you don't know."

I had imagined a lot of reasons why Wai Po had a problem with my performing. Maybe she thought it was too show-offy, or it took time away from my studies. Maybe she thought it would cost too much money. This was a reason I had never even considered.

"That is the way it was when I was a girl," she said.

"But this is different. This is America. No one thinks that way," I said. I also wanted to say it was a long time ago, but I didn't want Wai Po to think I was being rude.

"Maybe. Maybe not. It's just that I . . ." Wai Po glanced around the room, trying to find the right words. "I want you to have a good life, a good job. This is why I think it is good that your mom is going to law school. So she can have a better life, and that better life includes you. A lawyer is a secure, well-paying job."

"Well, then, you are probably glad that I won't be singing anymore," I said.

"No," said Wai Po. "You used to sing all day! Sing commercials, sing songs from the radio. Sing about the weather. Sing songs so I will make lunch for you and your friend, Oscar Mayer. Everything is a reason for a song. Now nothing is, and that is worse."

"You're so confusing sometimes," I told her. I wrapped my arms around her, feeling her birdlike boniness under the sweater.

"If you decide that you don't love singing anymore, that is fine," said Wai Po. "But I don't think that is the problem."

"How do you know?" I asked.

Wai Po looked right at me. As she got older, her eyes were getting lighter colored. Instead of being dark brown, they were bluish-gray. She answered my question with a question. "Why don't you want to watch *Star Search*?"

It would have been easier to say that *Star Search* was for babies, or that I could tell who was going to win. But when Mini turned on the TV, the truth was much harder. Of course I still wanted to go on *Star Search*. Even knowing that I would never get on didn't change that one bit.

What I said instead was, "It's stupid. It's just singing."

Wai Po didn't say anything, so I did the silence-filling thing again. "You lived through a war!" I said. "Singing just isn't that important."

"Who," asked Wai Po, "are you trying to convince?"

CHAPTER 26

SOMETHING MISSING

"I FEEL LIKE WE'RE GOING BACKWARD
here," said Mrs. Tyndall. "Something is still *missing*."

She was about to say more when a weird, whispery voice
stole across the stage. *Missing. Missing. Missing.*

Mrs. Tyndall stopped talking and held stock-still. "Do
you hear that?" she asked us.

I nodded, but the rest of the cast shook their heads.

She waited a few more moments, but there was no more
sound.

"Is someone in the booth?" asked Mrs. Tyndall.

No answer.

"Why don't you step out into the hallway and practice,"
said Mrs. Tyndall. She must have really been unnerved,
because she didn't like us to leave the auditorium. "David,

go with them." Being hoop wrangler had somehow given David a teacher-like status.

But it was Duncan who took over.

"I have an idea," he said. "Let's mix it up, and instead of having boys and girls singing, we'll have different parts of the group singing."

Duncan's idea made me nervous. I could hide easily in larger groups, but a smaller group would be a challenge.

"But we shouldn't sing too loud, right?" I said. "We're in the hallway."

Duncan gave me a weird look. "There's no one else here."

"But we don't want to attract attention," I said.

"The whole point of being in the musical is to attract attention," said Duncan. "Are you okay? Do you need a drink of water or something?"

Duncan divided us every way he could think of. The right side of the group sang, and then the left. The front sang, and then the back.

"Listen to each other," said Duncan. "We're supposed to sing as one."

Except when you're the one not singing, I thought. But no one seemed to notice.

We went back to the auditorium and took our usual places in the back.

"QUIETLY, ensemble," Mrs. Tyndall shouted.

Cheryl pulled out a piece of paper. I was sitting to her

right and saw her write *What was missing?* at the top. Then she handed the paper to her left. Then it went to Andy and Lila and Michael Spiers and Hallelujah. When it got to Duncan, who was sitting on my other side, I pulled out my pen, and he handed me the paper. I was going to write something smart, like enunciation. But when I looked down, there was my name, over and over, in six different types of handwriting.

Why didn't you sing? Duncan wrote.

How did you know I wasn't?

Because the group you're in should sound better than the group you're not in, he wrote.

Not anymore, I wrote back.

CHAPTER 27

ON THIS NIGHT

THE FIRST PASSOVER SEDER WAS
on Monday night, so I had to leave extra early from play rehearsal. I made my mom write a note, in case Mrs. Tyndall didn't believe me.

Please allow Lauren Horowitz to miss the end of rehearsal. Tonight is Passover, and we need her home in time for this important religious observance.

I could see her lawyerly touch, even in those two lines. "Can you add that it's a Jewish observance?" I asked.

"I'm sure she knows," said Mom. "That's just general knowledge."

"She may know it's a Jewish holiday, but she doesn't believe I'm Jewish," I said.

Mom looked at me for a long moment and then wedged the word *Jewish* above *religious* in her careful handwriting.

Mrs. Tyndall didn't say anything about that when I handed her the note, though. "It's never good to miss a rehearsal this close to the performance," she said. "But at least you're not the lead."

Thanks for reminding me, I thought.

Sometimes we have big seders, like when my aunt and uncle come to visit. But this year it was just the usual suspects.

I helped set the table and added the charoset and roasted egg to the seder place. They were kind of strange-looking, but they all belonged there.

We dressed up for our seders, but they were still pretty casual. Last year Hector and Tara came, because Mom thinks it is important to share the meal with other people, and to introduce them to things like matzoh ball soup. There's a line at the beginning that says, "Let all who are hungry come eat." That pretty much covers Hector.

This year she'd invited Gary, an intern from her office who was Jewish.

One of the parts at the beginning of the seder is called the four questions, where the youngest child asks four questions about the Passover holiday. Usually David does them with me, to keep me company. My stomach tightened up. The questions were usually sung. I went to David to see if he was still singing.

"But I had my bar mitzvah," he said.

"So?" I said.

"So I'm a man now," he said.

Not even close, I thought, but that would not have helped my case. "So?" I said again. "Does that mean after my bat mitzvah no one will do them?"

David thought about this.

"Besides," I said, "you like questions." In the end, he caved.

Before we started singing, I took a deep breath and hoped that sadness would not well up inside me and that I would not ruin Passover for everyone. I planned on keeping my voice low, letting David carry the music.

But something else happened. It felt familiar and comforting, like coming home after a long time away. I thought about all the kids who had sung these melodies and asked these questions before me, who were probably asking them right now. The song made me more than myself.

We took turns asking the questions in English.

They sound more complicated in Hebrew, in song, but the four questions are actually pretty basic questions about the holiday, like why, on this night, we eat matzoh instead of regular bread.

My dad liked to tell guests, especially when they weren't Jewish, that they could stop the seder any time to ask other questions. And the questions didn't just have to be about Passover, either.

This year, I had other questions, like why, on this night, was my best friend not my best friend anymore. And if I wasn't part of the Royal We, what was left? The Royal Me didn't sound right. Without Tara, I didn't feel royal. When she came to our Passover seder last year, she'd been polite enough to say she liked gefilte fish until I told her she didn't have to say that.

"Oh, good," she said. And everyone had laughed.

After we finished the first part of the service, and everyone had choked on the horseradish to be reminded of the bitterness of slavery, I helped Mom put out the first course, the gefilte fish Tara had secretly hated. It was in a sort of oval mound, and there were little bits of a clear, jellylike substance stuck to it. If I was a side dish, I hoped I was never that.

"Do you think this would be good in soup?" Wai Po said.

The questions she asked at Passover seder were usually about the food, like: "Don't you think we should tell Gary he doesn't have to eat the potato kugel if he doesn't like it?" Everyone turned and stared at Gary when she said that. Gary looked down at the heap of kugel on his plate and took a big bite.

Safta had made the kugel. Her questions were things like: "So, Gary, have you met any nice Jewish girls? I may know someone."

Gary's question was, "Do you need any help in the kitchen, Natalie?" His voice squeaked a little at the end.

While we were eating, I realized that Patsy asked a lot of questions in her songs. Some of her song titles were questions, like "Have You Ever Been Lonely?" and "How Can I Face Tomorrow?" Sometimes she had questions in her songs, like in "Walkin' After Midnight," she wonders if the man she loves is crying for her.

Big questions. Life-changing questions.

The thing about questions is, at some point you have to start thinking about the answers. Maybe my question shouldn't have been about what happened to the Royal We, but how to fix the Royal We. Or if I *wanted* to fix the Royal We at all.

CHAPTER 28

JUST TRYING TO BE FUNNY

FOR THE NEXT TWO WEEKS, IT WAS
like we were operating in parallel universes. Tara's universe
was at the front of the stage. Mine was at the back. Sometimes,
a portal opened up and we waved at each other through it.
But mostly, she stayed in her universe and I stayed in mine.

Cheryl's birthday was on Saturday, and she invited the
sixth-grade girls in the ensemble out to the movies at Oak
Faire Mall. "After the movie, we'll go to the food court," she
said. "My mom will treat for pizza."

I hadn't been to the movies in a while, as part of our plan
to save up for my bat mitzvah. My mom didn't see any point
in paying four dollars a ticket when the whole family could
rent a movie for one dollar. But she had to make an excep-
tion for a birthday party. "Meet me at Sears at nine," she said
as she dropped me off.

I checked my purse to make sure I still had Cheryl's present, a pack of soda-flavored lip glosses and a button I made her that said ENSEMBLE MEANS TOGETHER.

I saw Hallelujah and Lila in the lobby of the theater, and then Cheryl joined us.

I was looking forward to not thinking about the play and not singing. Just settling into the dark of a movie and being somewhere else for a while. Then a portal opened between universes, and Tara and Jennifer Gallagher walked in. Tara smiled and waved.

Tara and I had never shown up to the same event without knowing that the other would be there. In fact, we usually gave each other rides. But when Cheryl said she was inviting some of the girls in the ensemble, I had mentally cut out Tara. Now it felt as if I had done something wrong, like I'd been cheating.

We clumped around the ticket booth, taking turns buying our tickets. Lila and Cheryl went to get the popcorn.

Tara walked over as if nothing was wrong. "Hey," she said.

"Hey." She was wearing one of the buttons I'd made for her mom's campaign. "Nice button."

"Nothing but the best," said Tara. She moved to the front of the line and bought her ticket. We went in right away so we could all get seats together. I thought about my question from Passover, how to fix the Royal We, and called out to Tara.

"Sit over here," I said, pointing to the seat next to me, just as Tara started lowering herself between Jennifer and Lila. Tara smiled and shook her head slightly. Were Jennifer and Tara becoming a new Royal We? Now I had made an awkward extra seat in our row, trying to hold it for Tara. I put my jacket and purse on the empty seat, hoping no one would notice.

And then it got worse.

Sixteen Candles is about a girl whose family forgets her sixteenth birthday because her older sister is getting married. I'd heard other kids talking about it at school. It was supposed to be funny, which was what I told Hallelujah as the lights went down.

"As long as it's not horror," she said.

But it turned out to be a different kind of horror movie.

In the movie, the main character's grandparents bring a foreign exchange student with them named Long Duk Dong. I guess it was supposed to be a Chinese name, because people in the movie referred to him as a Chinaman, even though the actor was Japanese. At first, I was excited to see him up there on the big screen. But instead of being a real person, he was like a cartoon. A gong sounded after he talked or smiled.

Every time he appeared on-screen, everyone laughed, including my friends. I could make out Tara's laugh, even in the dark. They laughed when he said his lines in broken English. I was supposed to laugh, too, but all I wanted to do was leave. He wasn't the main character, so I kept hoping that every time he appeared on camera, it would be the last time. But he kept coming back, like a rash.

I wanted to jump into the movie and fix it. "Stop making fun of Long Duk Dong," I wanted Molly Ringwald's character to say. But she never really spoke to him, and maybe that was just as bad.

After the movie, Cheryl led the way to the food court and ordered two large cheese pizzas and Cokes for everyone. We snagged a long white table with someone else's old mustard on it, and Cheryl sat at the head. I took a seat at the other end.

"Can you imagine if Jake Ryan went to our school?" Cheryl said. Jake Ryan was the boy that Molly Ringwald's character had a crush on. "I bet he'd be playing Elvis instead of Ricky."

Jennifer said, "Sorry, I have to stay true to Rob Lowe."

"He wasn't even in the movie," Lila said.

"Can we talk about her dress?" said Hallelujah. "I'd love a dress like that." As Samantha, Molly wore a delicate pink bridesmaid's dress in her sister's wedding.

The happy chatter flowed around me. But I felt like I was coming down with food poisoning, even though we hadn't eaten anything yet.

I peeked at my watch. Eight fifteen. I wished I could get my mom to come sooner, but I was stuck.

A kid, maybe in fourth grade, came over to our table. He

smiled like he had some good news to tell us. I smiled back at him, hoping he'd do something so we'd stop talking about the movie.

"Ching chong," he shouted. His eyes narrowed, and he bared his teeth. "Long Duk Dong!" His voice was scratchy. "Donger." He started to run off, but then something stopped him.

Me.

I had this weird, out-of-body feeling, as if I were watching myself instead of acting. I was holding the back of his T-shirt. I saw his shirt stretch as he struggled to get away from me, but there was no pull of the cloth against my fingers. My hand was clenched in a fist.

"Lauren," said Hallelujah. "What are you doing?"

A man walked over. "Hey! Let go of my kid." His face was very red. "Blake, are you okay?"

I let go of the shirt, and Blake catapulted into his dad, then turned to face me, his breathing sharp and raw.

"He screamed at me." My voice sounded like it was coming from somewhere else.

"I just said the name of that guy from the movie," whined Blake.

"Aw, he was just fooling around," said the man.

"I am not Long Duk Dong," I said to him. "I am not the Donger. You don't go around shouting random names at people you don't know." Out of the corner of my eye, I could see the girls staring at me. I didn't care.

"It was a joke," said the man.

"He didn't say it like a joke," I said.

I took a step toward Blake and leaned closer to his level. "What made you think we would find this funny?" I asked him the question like a scientist, like how my dad told us to ask at the seder. *What made you think it was going to rain? Why did the apple fall down instead of up?* The boy looked at me, his gray eyes wide, and didn't say anything.

A crowd had started to form around us. If my mom were here, she would probably want to kill me for grabbing a kid I didn't know, for talking back to an adult. "I thought Orientals raised their kids to be respectful," said Blake's dad.

The truth was, I *had* been raised to be respectful, but I was too mad to care. "Why don't you raise yours that way, too?" I said.

The man stared at me for a second, too, and then gave me the finger. Then he stalked off, barely letting his son's feet touch the ground.

I sat back down at the table, not looking at anyone. I tried to take a sip of Coke, but my hands were shaking so much that the ice rattled.

"What," said Cheryl. "Just happened."

"Are you okay?" asked Tara. There was no question who the *you* was.

I nodded. I didn't want to ruin Cheryl's birthday. "Sorry," I said.

The table fell silent. I tried to take a bite of pizza, but my throat was too tight to swallow, so I just ended up chewing a tiny bite until nothing was left.

Jennifer said, "I'm sorry you're upset, but I think that kid was just trying to be funny. You didn't have to grab him."

There were some murmured noises of agreement. But Hallelujah, who was sitting next to me, said, "That was not the face of someone trying to be funny. I've seen that face."

Lila said, "Weren't you so scared that the dad was going to do something?"

I waited to hear Tara say something else. Anything to show that we were more connected than anyone at the table.

When she didn't, I reached into my purse and handed Cheryl's present to her. "I have to go meet my mom," I said. "Happy birthday."

I wandered around Sears in a daze. I started in the hardware department and then found myself in women's bras. I got out of there and went over to the toy department. When I was younger, this was my favorite place. I used to pretend that I was on a shopping spree, and would pick out what I would get with my money. The Barbie Dreamhouse was always high on the list. I also wanted one of those heads with makeup and hair you could style, but Mom said I was too young to think about makeup.

Out of the corner of my eye, I saw a familiar tan jacket over in the housewares section, and I started running. My legs couldn't go fast enough. I ran past the display of bath towels and a barbecue. Mom saw me just in time to open her arms and catch me as I fell into her.

I was safe. I was finally safe.

"What," she murmured, stroking my hair the way she did when I was little. "What happened? Tell me." She used to sing a lullaby for me when she stroked my hair, waiting for me to fall asleep. Like a lot of lullabies, it was a little weird. It's about a stranger, calling to a little rabbit to let the stranger in.

> *Xiao tu zi guai guai*
> *Good little rabbit*
> *Ba men kai kai*
> *Open the door*
> *Bu kai bu kai jiu bu kai*
> *Not opening the door*
> *Mama hui lai wo cai kai.*
> *I'll open the door when Mom comes back.*

CHAPTER 29

A REAL PERSON

MAYBE BEING MAD MADE ME braver. Or maybe I was ready this time. We sat in the car in the parking lot, and I told Mom everything. Not just the movie and Blake. I told her about the audition and Mrs. Tyndall and Pleasant Valley and Tara. I told her about how Mrs. Tyndall had seemed so reasonable, but now it didn't seem right, even if I couldn't say why.

"She said she wanted the audience to be transported to Pleasant Valley, but they wouldn't be able to do that if I was Brenda Sue," I explained. "It would be 'confusing.'"

"Because Brenda Sue is supposed to look a certain way," said Mom.

"Right. And not like me," I said. "Like Tara."

"I bet that makes it twice as hard," said Mom. "When it's your best friend."

"You have no idea."

Mom put her arm around me and didn't say anything. It felt good. Sometimes you don't need a reaction; you just need someone to be with you while the terribleness happens.

"I should just be happy for Tara, right? And I should be happy that we're in the play together. I should be happy I made the ensemble. I'm lucky. Lots of people tried out and didn't make the play at all. I've made some really good friends in the ensemble. It was a good thing. But . . ."

But.

"You're human," said Mom. "And you're not always going to get the part you want. But when you lose, you want it to be for the right reasons. I don't think the reason Mrs. Tyndall gave you was a right reason."

"Maybe it was," I said. "I mean, that movie. Maybe people would think of me the same way. A joke. Maybe Mrs. Tyndall is doing me a favor."

"That's not how you fix things," said Mom. "By hiding yourself. By letting people see less of you. Those men in Detroit, they didn't see Vincent Chin as a real person. He was a symbol. And that judge didn't value Vincent's life like a real person's, either."

Thinking about Vincent Chin used to make me feel

scared. I wanted to have reasons to be separate from him. But now I felt differently.

"Is Vincent Chin why you want to go to law school?" I asked.

"He's one reason," she said. "But I have two other very good reasons. David. And you."

CHAPTER 30

APPEASING THE THEATER GHOST

"DO YOU HAVE A PICTURE OF VINCENT
Chin?" I asked Mom.

On the way home, we stopped at her office. I hadn't been there in a long time, though it was pretty much as I had remembered. Her desk was very orderly, and she had put up pictures of David's bar mitzvah, including one of our whole family. Mom pulled out a manila folder from a drawer; it had clippings of newspapers about Vincent's case. A couple of the articles had his picture.

He had the kind of hair that David wanted, thick and parted in the middle. He was older than me and David, but younger than my parents. He looked friendly.

My mom turned on the Xerox machine to make me a copy of the newspaper article. "We're allowed to make copies for personal use," she told me. "As long we don't get carried away." She made extra copies, just in case.

When we got home, I pulled out my button-making kit and got it right the first try. Vincent's smiling face looked back at me from the center of the button.

At lunch on Monday, Duncan came up to me and said, "Why are you wearing a picture of your brother?"

I looked down at the button and then back up at Duncan. "That's not David."

Duncan took a step toward me and peered at the button. "You're right," he said.

"Duh," I said.

"Jordy said David ran away from home and you were wearing his picture in his honor. Or that maybe he needed a kidney."

"That's insane! David was on the bus this morning. And he has B lunch."

"You could have B lunch and still need a kidney," he said. "That's good, though. I was wondering who else Mrs. Tyndall could get to be hoop wrangler."

I debated taking the button off, but then Duncan said, "So who is it? Is that a Chinese movie star?"

I shook my head and looked down at the button. I told Duncan about Vincent Chin. I tried to remember all the details that my mom told me, about how the guys who murdered Vincent hadn't served a day in prison.

"My uncle says stuff about the Japanese," Duncan said. "But Vincent Chin was Chinese."

That's what I had said, when my mom had first told me the story. But now I understood what the point was. "Vincent was an American," I said. "He deserved justice."

"Yeah," said Duncan. He wiped his mouth with the sleeve of his rugby shirt. I think he was nervous.

Duncan took a step toward me, and for a moment, I thought he was going to try to put his arm around me or something, and I wasn't sure how I felt about that. But he was taking a closer look at Vincent.

"He looks happy," Duncan said. "I used to think I could tell that people were dead from how they looked in their photos, but then I realized that it was just because they were old people in black-and-white photos, and chances were, they were dead."

"That's weird, Dunk," I said.

"Little kids have weird thoughts."

"I used to think that it was impossible to stay up until midnight. Like, it was physically impossible," I said.

"I used to worry about getting sucked down the drain at the end of my bath. My mom would always yell at me for jumping out of the tub before she was ready with my towel."

"I always wanted my mom to put me in the dryer at the end of my bath. I would get so mad that she wouldn't do it! I kept thinking that if she would just do it once, she'd see I was a genius."

Duncan started laughing. When he laughed, his face

turned red, and he doubled over from laughing so hard. It was impossible not to join in. Other kids started turning around and staring at us. I waited for him to stop.

"The thing is," I said, "my mom says now that I know, I can't let things stay the same."

"So . . . the button."

"The button that no one noticed but you."

"Maybe you could make one for me. Maybe that would help."

"Maybe people will think you've joined the search party looking for David," I said.

"But if they ask about it," he said, "I can tell them about Vincent. I'll tell them he also belonged in an American town." Duncan was making a reference to the song from the musical. "You do, too, you know."

"Not to Mrs. Tyndall."

"But her opinion isn't the only one that matters, right?"

"Right." I wouldn't ever be Mrs. Tyndall's all-American girl, but maybe I'd just be my own.

"Okay, ensemble," Mrs. Tyndall said, "I don't think I need to remind you that we are two weeks out. You should be getting better. Not worse. From the top."

She clapped her hands and told us to get out our hoops. "Ensemble hoopers on stage left should start their hoops counterclockwise. Ensemble hoopers on stage right should start their hoops clockwise."

Duncan and Andy got a few spins around before their hoops clattered to the floor. Max pretended to start but then caught the hoop when Mrs. Tyndall looked away. "Maybe she should just see if she can swap some people," Hallelujah whispered to me.

"Meanwhile," Mrs. Tyndall was saying, "our Brenda Sue needs to be right up here, showing everyone how it's done. Brenda Sue, you just take this hoop and—*RAAAAOW!*" Mrs. Tyndall let out a terrible scream and fell to the floor. We all dropped our hoops and ran over.

The ghost, I thought. *The ghost got Mrs. Tyndall!*

Mrs. Tyndall rolled slowly onto her back, clutching her knees. "It's my back," she gasped. She had tears in her eyes. For once, she looked small, lying on the floor while we stood over her.

"I'll go find someone," said Michael. He looked upset, like this was his fault.

Hector stood there, probably trying to imagine what ambulances looked like in the 1950s.

"Oh no, oh no," said Tara.

"Don't flip your wig," said Hector, though I could tell by his voice that he was flipping his.

Mrs. Tyndall closed her eyes and took a few deep breaths. Then she opened her eyes and looked at us. "Well? Why are you all just standing here?"

"Um, because this is a medical emergency?" said Cheryl.

"I'm not dying," said Mrs. Tyndall. "This would be a

good time to remind you all of the most important credo in show business. The show must go on. This is what it means to be committed. I had a girl sprain her ankle in act one, and she didn't tell anyone until the show was over. I had a Romeo who threw up in the middle of the balcony scene because he was coming down with the flu. He ducked behind the balcony, and no one was the wiser. This"—she pointed to herself—"should not stop you."

The ensemble exchanged glances. We had problems with Mrs. Tyndall, but this was, admittedly, impressive. Michael came in with Mr. Hoban, the principal.

Mr. Hoban knelt down next to Mrs. Tyndall. "How are we doing, Edna? Do we need to call someone?"

"I will need help getting up," she said. "After the rehearsal. And I could use some Tylenol. Now. I think I have some in my purse."

Mr. Hoban got the purse and carried it back across the stage. Then he started looking through it, which I thought was pretty brave of him.

Mrs. Tyndall gestured toward us. "Ensemble, perform 'Normal American Boy' for Mr. Hoban."

Lila looked at me. "It's the principal."

I nodded.

"We haven't performed for anyone outside of the cast and crew. And Mr. Shea," she said. "We need to get this right. We need you."

I waited for a moment to see if the sad, heavy feelings were coming. But there was something different. Not like Passover, but something else. Anticipation. Hope. Daring. That was what my mom and Duncan had been trying to tell me. People needed to see me. They needed to hear me, too.

I nodded. I could do this. We could do this.

Tiffany walked over. "You've got this," she said. She raised her arms and counted us off.

I opened my mouth, and the notes lifted out of it. I sang for Mr. Hoban. I sang for the ensemble and for Vincent and for Patsy. And I sang for myself.

But down deep inside, where your feelings abide,
you're a normal American boy.

"That was great!" Mr. Hoban said to us. "I can't wait for the show." I was pretty sure that was a line out of the principal handbook, like, *Always say something positive about the student production.* But I felt like he was talking to me.

Duncan nudged me. "The theater ghost must have been appeased. We sounded pretty good."

"Yeah," I said. Maybe it was a different kind of ghost that had been quieted. One in my head. The ghost of not-supposed-to. Because singing was what I was supposed to be doing. My face felt numb, possibly from smiling.

"Singing is the language of the soul." That's what Grandpa Joe used to say. That's what it felt like: like my soul was singing.

CHAPTER 31

ON THE AIR

MY NEW BUTTON HAD A PICTURE and the words WHAT HAPPENED TO VINCENT CHIN? This time, lots of kids asked about it since 1) it asked a question they didn't know the answer to and 2) they could see that my brother had not run away and did not need a kidney and 3) Duncan was wearing one, too.

Every time I told Vincent's story, I felt stronger. It was like we were making a promise not to allow things like that to happen again.

Then I went to science. We had a sub who didn't care what we did as long as we finished our worksheet on electricity, so Tara came over to my table.

"Guess what?" she said.

"What?" For a second I thought she was going to talk

about the movie and what happened afterward. But no one was saying anything. It was like they had taken an extra-large eraser and wiped it all away.

"I get to be in the regional oratory competition after all!"

"Wait. I thought you said you came in second."

"I did. But Allison Crockett, who came in first, has to be in her uncle's wedding, and they are not rescheduling that for the oratory competition, so I get to go in her place. Look at this." She handed me a picture of a pale-pink Laura Ashley dress with tiny flowers on it. "My mom said she would get me a new dress."

"It's beautiful," I said. "And getting to go is an excellency." I did not sing the word. We were both being polite, which did not feel normal. I pointed at my button. "I have my topic for next year's oratory."

"Oh yeah," said Tara. "I heard some kids talking about it."

"You mean him. Vincent Chin."

"Yeah, that. All of that."

I tried not to feel irritated. Vincent Chin wasn't a *that*. He was a person.

"Did they tell you that he was about to get married? Or that the men who—"

"Yeah."

I didn't say anything for a moment, trying to pull myself together. I thought Tara would feel the way I did, but instead, she was like a resistor. Resistors are used to reduce current

205

flow. I had the electricity of Vincent's story flowing through me, but she would not allow it.

"I don't know if it would make a good oratory topic, honestly," said Tara. "You didn't know him."

"People do oratories on people they don't know all the time," I said. "Lila did hers on Harriet Tubman, remember? And people are always quoting Einstein."

"But because of how Vincent looks, people are going to think it's personal."

"It is personal," I said. "What happened to Vincent was because of how he looks." I waited to see if Tara made the connection, the last link in the chain of thought.

She didn't. "I'm just saying," she said, "based on my experience at county—"

"I don't care about that," I said.

"I'm only trying to help," said Tara. "You said you had a topic for oratory, and I'm not sure it's the best one. You're not mad, are you?"

The bell rang, saving me from having to answer. But I *was* mad. It felt like Tara was deliberately missing the point. Maybe the Royal We was over.

At play practice, Mrs. Tyndall asked us to solicit advertisements for the program as a way to pay for paint and props like Tara's wooden hoop.

"Pair up," she said. "If you get two ads each, we'll be in business."

I looked over at Tara. After our last conversation, it didn't seem like we would want to be partners. But then Mrs. Tyndall said: "Brenda Sue and Theodore, I have special plans for you."

"My mom says she'll take out an ad. Buchanan for mayor," said Tara. "Half a page."

Cheryl grabbed my hand. "You and me," she said.

I already had an idea of where to go: To a Tee.

And I had another idea, too: WTRY. I still owed Nashville Nick an apology.

Wai Po was not a fan of students going to strangers to sell advertising.

"I will be glad when this play is over," she said. But she let me go.

We started with WTRY, which wasn't far from Cheryl's house. We walked to the end of the street, where the houses stopped and the commercial area started. There was a weedy lot, a Putt-Putt golf course, and a low building with the WTRY letters gleaming on a brick wall. Somehow I had imagined the building would be more glamorous.

We walked through the field and then walked around the building to the front door. We could hear music playing as we walked in the front doors. There was a place for a receptionist, but it was empty. There was also a big glass window that looked into the DJ booth. Inside there was a tall, slightly overweight black man with a mustache and beard who looked like he was testing one of the dials.

"Excuse me," Cheryl said. She waved both her hands to try to attract his attention.

He came out of the booth.

"Well," he said, "the record promotions team gets younger and younger."

"We're not promoting a record," Cheryl said.

"We're promoting a play," I said. "At Eisenhower Junior High. We're selling advertising."

He stuck out his hand. "Nashville Nick," he said.

This was Nick? But it wasn't even time for his show. In my head, Nash was a white man with a flannel shirt and a cowboy hat. Then I caught myself; it was another supposed-to.

"I'm Cheryl," said Cheryl. "This is Lauren."

"Good to meet you both."

It was the voice I'd listened to so many times; I had just imagined it coming out of somebody else. I thought about pretending I'd never heard of him before. Maybe I could just leave an apology note on the front desk.

"Nice to meet you, too," I said.

Nash tilted his head to one side. "Lauren? Patsy Cline Lauren?"

I was too surprised to keep pretending. "How did you know?"

"I never forget a voice," said Nash. "That's my job."

"I should have called you back," I said. "After the Patsy thing. I'm sorry."

"I'm sorry, too," he said. "I shouldn't have assumed you knew. Are you okay now?"

I shrugged and wondered how much he remembered from our conversation. DJs talked to a lot of people. I thought about all the stuff people told Top 40 DJ Casey Kasem for those long-distance dedications. Stuff about mistakes and lost love and not fitting in.

Nash made a little circling motion, pointing at me. "You weren't what I was expecting."

I wasn't sure if it was because I wasn't what he pictured when I said I was Jewish, or because he thought I was older.

I figured I'd cover all the bases. "I'm twelve," I said. "And my mom is Chinese." Maybe the assumption part wasn't the bad part. It was what you did with it that mattered. I had made assumptions, too. "I thought you were white."

"I get that a lot," said Nash.

"People always think my parents are married," said Cheryl.

He nodded. "So about this play," he said.

"It's a production of *Shake It Up*," I said. "It's a musical. And for just fifteen dollars we'll put your name in the program."

"It doesn't sound country," he said. "But that's quite a bargain. Would you like to sing part of a song on the radio so our listeners will know what it's like?"

That sounded like free advertising. And it would make the ensemble look pretty good, maybe better than the stars.

"How much do you want to hear?" I said.

"Just a chorus," he said. "Cowgirl Connie left early today, and I'm trying to fill up her time."

Cheryl looked at me. "We could do some lines from 'Jumping through Hoops,'" she said. I nodded.

"Okay," he said. "I'll give you the intro. On three." He held up his fingers. "All right, music fans, this isn't exactly country, but some members of the Eisenhower Junior High cast of *Shake It Up* are right here in my studio. Ladies? Will you sing us a little bit of what we can expect from this show?"

Cheryl and I looked at each other, and I nodded. The verses were short, so we sang two of them together, our voices blending.

"May eighteenth and nineteenth at Dwight D. Eisenhower," Cheryl said. "Be there or be square."

Nash nodded, and leaned into the microphone. "Coming up next, I've got 'Mountain of Love' to help get you through the long afternoon."

"That's nice," I said as the first few notes bounced out of the speaker.

"That's Charley Pride," said Nash. He held up the record album. Charley Pride was black, too. I'd never seen any black country singers before.

"Do you have any Chinese Jewish country singers?" I asked.

Nash looked at me. "Well, I've got one right here."

"No, I mean a real singer."

"You're a real singer," said Cheryl.

"I wish," I said.

"Wishing on a star won't make you one," Nash said. "You know, Patsy Cline got her start when she sang on a local radio station."

"I wouldn't know what to sing," I said. I wondered if Cowgirl Connie would be mad that I sang during her show.

"Sing Patsy!" said Cheryl.

"I can't sound like Patsy, not the way I want to," I said.

"You can sing anything you want," said Nash. "As long as it's country."

Besides Patsy, I wasn't sure I knew any country songs well enough to sing on the radio. I didn't think Nash's fans would appreciate "She'll Be Comin' Round the Mountain." Other than that, the only thing I could do was the theme songs from *The Beverly Hillbillies* and *The Andy Griffith Show*, and the last one didn't count because it was just whistling. That was something else we weren't allowed to do during play rehearsal. Whistling backstage was bad luck. But I wasn't in the theater anymore.

"What about 'Country Roads'?" I said. "Wouldn't a song with the word *country* count as country music?" We had learned it in music last year.

Nash shrugged. "John Denver is more folk than country, but I just let you sing a song from a musical, so there you go."

"Let me . . . let me run through it once," I said.

"Take all the time you need."

I grabbed Cheryl's arm, and we walked into the bath-room. I looked like a TV ad for Dramamine, the *before* part, when the person in the ad is green.

"I'm not sure about this," I said, splashing cold water on my face.

"You can't complain there are no Chinese Jewish coun-try singers if you turn down the chance to be one."

"I know," I said.

"Put up or shut up," said Cheryl. She folded her arms.

"You're awfully mean for a nice person," I told her.

"Thank you. That is one of the nicest things anyone has ever said to me."

"I just thought getting a chance at being a star would look different," I said. "With a record or something."

"As my mom says, sometimes you're living the dream and you don't even know it." I thought that was a pretty good observation. I thought about the advice Tara would give me, if she was with me. It felt weird to have such a big excellency without her.

"Okay," I said. I took some deep breaths. "I'm not going to throw up. At least during the song." We went over the song a few times, just to make sure I knew all the words.

I walked back into the studio while Cheryl went to call her mom. Nash had pulled up another chair next to his, and he gestured for me to sit down. He handed me a pair of headphones and then drew the microphone near me. The song "He Stopped Loving Her Today" was playing.

I felt dizzy. I felt wonderful.

Nash let the song finish and then turned to the mic. "Ladies and gentlemen, we're taking a break from our regularly scheduled program to bring you a special treat. As you know, I'm always on the lookout for new artists to share with you, but this one might be the youngest I've met." Nash looked at me and winked. "In the studio with me today is a young lady who I think has a great career ahead of her. Here's Lonesome Lauren, and she's going to sing 'Country Roads.'"

This was it. I couldn't sing sitting down, so I stood up and leaned down toward the microphone. I closed my eyes and let the opening guitar notes play in my head. Then I joined in, letting my voice sail over the radio.

"Country Roads" is about going home and the feelings you get when you're heading there. It says it's about West Virginia, but my music teacher said John Denver could have meant Virginia, because we have the Blue Ridge Mountains and most of the Shenandoah River, and West Virginia has only a trickle.

The song itself feels like a ride down a road, smooth and rolling, with a few hills to keep things interesting. The words and melody flow into each other, and by the time you hit the chorus and the note that goes with *yesterday*, you feel like you're flying. In my mind, I played a music video with the song, seeing fields and trees on the way home.

When the song ended, I opened my eyes. Cheryl and

Nash were staring at me. Nash turned to the mic. "We're going to change our call letters to WOW," he said. "Because all I can say is 'Wow.' Good job, Lonesome Lauren." A light on the board came on. "Oh, we have a caller. Hello, WTRY."

"Hi, Nash, it's Audrey. I'm calling about that young lady you just had on."

"Oh, hi, Audrey. Yes, what would you like to say?"

"Well, if I were John Denver, I'd be absolutely furious about the way Laura sang that song."

What? I grabbed my stomach, and Cheryl slid the trash can over to me. I'll bet you could hear it on the air.

"Her name is Lauren," said Nash politely. But he hovered a finger over the button marked MUTE. Audrey kept talking.

"Well, she made that song sweeter and lovelier than even John Denver did. And I didn't think anyone could do that."

"Agreed," said Nash.

"Just tell her next time to sing some real country," Audrey said.

CHAPTER 32

CONFESSIONS BY THE RADIO

CHERYL AND I WALKED OVER TO 7-Eleven to buy snacks to celebrate what Cheryl called my "on-air debut." We sat on the curb and talked. She told me she only saw her dad once a year because he lived in Alaska. "Most of the time, it's just me and my mom," she said.

I told her about my grandmothers.

"Want to trade?" said Cheryl, taking a bite of her Ho Ho, which we had dubbed the official snack of the on-air debut, not to be confused with Yoo-hoo, the official drink of the on-air debut. She licked chocolate icing off her finger.

She was joking, I knew. But I answered honestly. "No," I said. "But you can join us!"

I was supposed to go straight home after spending time with Cheryl, but I decided to take a detour. It wasn't that far out of the way, I reasoned. The path was as familiar as the path to my own home.

Tara answered the door.

"Hey," I said.

"Hey," she said. "Are you here for the button money? My mom's been asking." She turned away from the door and yelled, "Mo-o-om! Lauren's here for the button money."

The thing was, I wasn't there for the button money. I was there because even though Cheryl and I were becoming really good friends, there was also the Royal We, and the first person I wanted to tell everything to was still Tara.

Mrs. Buchanan came to the front door. "Well, don't just stand on the front step like a stranger! Come in, Lauren."

"I'm kind of busy," said Tara. But she pushed open the screen door. We stood in the front hall, looking at each other. Mrs. Buchanan got out her checkbook and wrote me a check. Their house was usually as neat as the furniture show-room at Grand Piano. Tara and I used to go there together to get the free Cokes they offered you if you were looking for a dining room set. But now the Buchanans' kitchen table was covered with papers and half-filled legal pads. Tara and I watched her mom go upstairs.

I tried to figure out a way to tell Tara about what had just happened, but that would involve telling her I really did like country music. But Tara spoke first.

"So I guess you're famous now," she said.

"Me?"

"Congratulations." She reached out her hand and shook mine, like we were meeting for the first time.

"You heard?" I said.

"I may or may not have gotten a call from the radio station, telling me to turn on my radio."

I didn't know whether to feel proud or embarrassed.

"So you DO like country music," she said.

"Yes," I said. "Some. What do you think?"

"When you sing it, it's great," she said.

"Thanks, though I've been told that 'Country Roads' isn't really country."

It would be so easy to pretend that this was why I came over, I thought. To talk about music. But I was tired of pretending. I wanted things to be real between us, which meant providing honest answers.

"You know how you asked me if I was mad?" I said. "About Vincent Chin? I was. I'm still mad, kind of. Really."

Normally when you tell someone you're mad at them, the tension immediately goes up. But this time, it was like opening a window, letting out the old air and bringing fresh air. Tara nodded.

"You hate me for getting the lead," said Tara. "Right?"

I paused. "I hate that I never had a shot at it." I took a deep breath and pushed myself to be honest, more honest. "Also: My middle name isn't weird."

I was worried that Tara would say I was making a big deal out of nothing, but then I realized, it was a big deal. To me.

"I thought . . . because you always say . . ." Tara's words tumbled over one another, like socks in the dryer. "I shouldn't have said that."

I nodded, feeling uncomfortable and better all at the same time.

"I could talk to Mrs. Tyndall about doing musicals where you could have a bigger part," Tara volunteered.

"There's only one that would work for her," I said, thinking of Hector's suggestion of *South Pacific*.

"So let's do that one!"

"I want more than one," I said. "I want to be anything."

Tara's face fell. "Sometimes, I wish we'd never tried out."

"I know," I said.

"Like Vincent Chin. You never even mentioned him, and now I feel like I'm responsible."

"I never said you were responsible." One of the few Chinese words I knew was for America. Mei guo. Beautiful country. It was hard to hold Vincent and mei guo in my heart at the same time.

"Vincent Chin was an American," I said. "So am I. We belong here."

"I know that," said Tara.

"Other people need to know it, too," I said. "Like certain people who think a Chinese Jewish American girl in an all-American town is confusing."

Tara's eyes widened slightly. "I changed my mind," she said. "I'm glad that we tried out. We can fix it."

218

"We haven't been 'we' in a long time."

"Well, we're back," said Tara.

"The Royal We," I said.

Ten days before the play, everyone had costumes except for the ensemble.

"Ensemble, check your parents' closets," advised Mrs. Tyndall. "Maybe they have something that looks like it came from the 1950s."

"We should all check our parents' closets," said Tara. "Bring in extras if you have them." The Royal We included the cast.

"I wonder if I can finish this in time?" Safta had offered the imitation Nudie suit shirt, which she was still working on. Wai Po had decided to make matching pants. "You can wear a different shirt if hers doesn't work out," she said.

"What's not to work out?" said Safta. "I'm almost done." She had brought her project and Mini over to settle in for a long afternoon of sewing. "I've planned out the rhinestones, and I have just enough left so that . . ." She looked around her, lifting up pillows. "Hmmmm."

"Why are you hmmmm-ing?" asked Wai Po.

"There were a few rhinestones left, and now I can't find them," said Safta. "Did you take them?"

"Nobody took them," said Wai Po.

Safta looked around the room and her eyes settled on Bao Bao.

"Bao Bao did not eat the rhinestones!" said Wai Po. "That's not food."

"A dog will eat anything," Safta said.

Out of the corner of my eye, I saw a glimmer. I turned my head just in time to see Mini stick out her tongue and flick a glittery rhinestone into her mouth.

———————————

According to the vet, Dr. Sachs, Mini would probably be fine. "As long as it's small and doesn't block the digestive tract," she told Safta, "they will pass." That was a nice way of saying that Mini would poop them out.

"Your smart cat ate rocks," Wai Po said, petting Bao Bao.

In spite of the vet's assurances, Safta still looked worried when she hung up the phone. Then she started going around the house, closing the toilets.

"What are you doing?" I asked.

"I need to make sure Mini poops out all the rhinestones," Safta said. "Until then, she can't use the toilet."

"You are going to go through Mini's poop and look for rhinestones?"

"What else can I do?" said Safta.

Wai Po was trying not to smile.

Safta pointed at Wai Po. "When Mini is here, you'll have to keep a close eye on Bao Bao so he won't eat her poop."

Wai Po opened her mouth and closed it.

"It is the least I can do," she said.

CHAPTER 33

AN UNEARTHLY SOUND

SAFTA WANTED TO GO TO THE department store to find some real cat toys for Mini. David was on poop watch, so I went with Safta to see if I could find any new clothes that looked 1950s. We stopped in the men's department to get my dad some new undershirts, and that's where we saw Rabbi Doug.

"Rabbi," said Safta. "How are you?"

Please don't be buying underwear. Please don't be buying underwear, I thought. But Rabbi Doug was just getting a pair of tube socks.

"Just fine," said Rabbi Doug. "I should be asking you the same question. I haven't seen you at services lately. Or Hebrew school." Before I could make up an excuse, he said, "Your mother told me about the play. Are you keeping up?"

Our Hebrew school class met twice a week, but I'd missed

a number of the Wednesday classes when Mrs. Tyndall had called play rehearsal.

"I'll be back soon," I said.

He smiled. "In the meantime, there are other ways to feel spiritual," he said. "Music. A walk."

"I've been listening to Jewish music," I said, forgetting, for a minute, that Patsy wasn't Jewish anymore. "And I walk to school most days."

"I hope you know the Aleinu as well as you know your lines."

I nodded. I had learned that one in third grade.

"We'll make sure she practices, Rabbi," said Safta.

He nodded and held up a pair of tube socks with the colors of the Miami Dolphins. "What do you think?"

"Good," I said. I wondered where he had gotten them. Mrs. Tyndall had suggested thick white socks, cuffed at the ankle, rolled-up jeans, and a white T-shirt. That's what Cheryl and Hallelujah were wearing. I guessed that's what I would be wearing, too.

Right before dress rehearsals, Mrs. Tyndall gave us a big lecture about theater etiquette while lying down on the stage. She had gotten an old megaphone from the school so we could all hear her.

"Do NOT say 'good luck!'" she said. "You can say 'break a leg.'"

"Do NOT ever say '*M-A-C-B-E-T-H*!' You can say 'the Scottish play.'"

"You mean *Macbeth*?" said Andy.

"I spelled it for a reason!" shouted Mrs. Tyndall, though I was pretty sure none of us would have thought of saying *Macbeth* until she said it.

"Do not whistle onstage! Do not clap onstage! This can cause confusion and miscues.

"Keep your costumes neat and tidy. Do not leave them lying around!"

Mrs. Tyndall had a lot of rules, and none of them were for bringing good luck. They were for warding off bad luck.

The school auditorium wasn't big enough for the entire school, so we only performed for the eighth graders and some seventh graders. Even then, it was pretty crowded; some of the teachers had to stand. This was why I was surprised to see Safta sitting in the back.

"What are you doing here?" No one else's grandparents were there.

"You can't take photos during a regular performance, so I asked if I could come for the dress rehearsal," said Safta. She held up her camera and waved it around. "Did you know that your principal grew up with my cousin's best friend's business partner? Small world."

Poor Mr. Hoban. He never knew what hit him. He

probably also did not know that Safta's photography was best known for its close-ups of her thumbs and her ability to cut off heads at any range.

When Safta put her camera down, I noticed that she did not have her regular purse with her. She had her cat-carrying bag.

I lowered my voice so the people milling around us wouldn't hear. "You didn't bring Mini, did you?"

"I had to because of the you-know-what."

My mind started to run through all the terrible things that could happen. Mini could pee or poo in the carrier and then stink up the whole theater. Safta could sit next to someone who was allergic to cats, and they could start sneezing uncontrollably. I decided to borrow a trick from Tiffany.

"Excuse me," I said, gesturing to the students sitting around Safta. "I'm taking a poll on allergies. Is anyone here allergic to milk? Grass?" I paused. "Cats?"

It turns out that most people will participate in polls just because they're bored. In Safta's immediate area, there was one kid who was allergic to grass and two kids allergic to milk, but that was it.

I let out a sigh of relief. I had at least prevented the worst of it.

The first act was a quasi-disaster. Hector forgot a whole stanza in his song, which kind of threw off the hoopers. And the doorknob came off in Tara's hand when she went to her father's store, but she did a great job of playing it off. "Father," she said, "the shop is in need of some upgrades." And the audience laughed right along.

Then, in the second act, weird things started happening.

During the show, we kept the ghost light turned off in the wings. But during Tara's solo, "Circling through Time," the light came on. Then went off. On. Off. On. Off.

Mrs. Tyndall shielded her eyes and stared menacingly up at the light booth. I could see one of the guys make the universal gesture for "we don't know what's happening."

"It's the ghost!" whispered Michael.

"There's probably a more rational reason," said Duncan. But he didn't sound completely convinced.

After Tara's solo ended, the light stopped flickering. But then a few minutes later, there was the distinct sound of movement up in the rafters. Something getting knocked over.

I ran over to Tara when her solo ended. "Did you see the ghost?"

Tara shook her head. "No, but there is definitely a weird vibe out there. Right before I went onstage, it felt like someone had brushed up against me, even though no one was there."

I shivered. I still hadn't made up my mind if ghosts were real or not. Every Passover, we waited for the spirit of Elijah to come in and drink the wine from a glass we left on the table, but that wasn't the same.

Then, during the scene of the meeting of Mothers United for Decency, a strange sound started.

"No son of mine will ever . . ." said Kelli Ann in her best mom voice.

"Arreeewww!"

Kelli Ann swallowed and finished the line. Sort of. "No son of mine will put a hip in that hoop!"

The sound was unearthly, the sound of torment and fear. The audience began to shift and murmur in their seats. We were supposed to go to intermission, but the mood was weird, uncertain.

Then it happened. From above the stage, something moved, but not in any way that a human could. The lights caught a flash of movement and the sound of running. Someone screamed.

"Ghost!"

It all made sense now. The flashing light. The moaning. And now this. The truth is not always pretty.

I darted forward. "It's not a ghost," I said. "It's a cat with a rhinestone problem."

And then the lights went out.

"I can't believe that you let Mini get out of the bag," I said to Safta.

"I didn't let her. She's just so clever that she managed to unzip the bag without me noticing," said Safta. I wondered if Safta ever bragged about me as much as she bragged about Mini. We were standing in the lobby, with Safta holding the still-empty bag.

The show did not go on.

"You would think," I said. "After taking Bao Bao into the hospital." Right before David's bar mitzvah, we had to take Wai Po to the emergency room. Safta and David snuck in Bao Bao to cheer her up, which was a good idea right up to the point when Bao Bao got loose.

"What?" said Safta. "Everything turned out fine."

"Well, now we have to figure out where Mini went," I said. "I just hope that she stayed in the auditorium."

"That's why you made the call, isn't it?" asked Safta.

At that moment, Wai Po came walking up to the school with Bao Bao on a leash. "Yes," I said. "Yes, it is."

I figured that if one creature on earth could figure out where Mini was, it would be Bao Bao. He was always sniffing her and following her around. Mini just had a bit of a head start this time.

The lights were still not working, so Tiffany found some flashlights. She gave one to Mrs. Tyndall, who was lying down on the stage in the dark. She gave Bao Bao two formal, awkward pats. "I hope he finds her soon. Good dog."

We started off in the seats, showing Bao Bao where Mini had last been. We made circles of lights on the seats. He sniffed around the chair and Safta held out the bag.

"Find Mini!" we told him.

I'm sure Bao Bao was doing his best. He certainly enjoyed the attention, and the dark didn't bother him a bit. Bao Bao made his way down to the stage, and then went back up the stairs to the lobby. Then he decided to go backstage. We went past the racks of clothes and David's special hoop setup. We looked around the motorcycle for Elvis. We peeked in the shelves that made up Brenda Sue's father's toy store.

"The cat could be anywhere," said David.

I looked at the clock. We had been searching almost an hour. A cold breath of air blew across the back of my neck, and it suddenly occurred to me that just because we knew about Mini didn't mean there wasn't a ghost. There could be a ghost and Mini.

Bao Bao sat down and started to bark.

"Where's the kitty? Find the kitty!" I said, trying to get him to stand back up.

"He must be tired," said Tara sympathetically.

"He doesn't know what he's doing," said Safta. "I hope you brought that can of cat food that I asked for."

"Found," said Wai Po. She pointed her flashlight into the rafters. And there, amid the rigging, two green eyes looked back at us. "Bao Bao is a hero!"

With a lot of coaxing and some cat food, Mini came down. "I'm glad this ended well," said Mrs. Tyndall from the floor. "But honestly, Lauren, I expected so much more from you."

"Me?" I said. "I didn't do anything. Safta brought Mini, not me."

"But she was here at your behest," said Mrs. Tyndall.

"You cannot behest her into doing anything," said Wai Po, nodding at Safta.

"Lauren did not know that Mini and I were here," said Safta. "Until we came."

Mrs. Tyndall looked up at my grandmothers. "I'm sure you're both very proud of Lauren." They both nodded. "But she has also been quite disruptive at times. She clearly craves the spotlight."

"She clearly deserves it," said Safta before I could stop her.

Then, almost as if they had planned it, Safta and Wai Po turned and marched up the aisle of the auditorium, like two lions, side by side.

I went into the bathroom with Tara so we could take off our makeup.

"Those stripes aren't very 1950s," Tara said, looking at my hair in the mirror. Even though it had been a few weeks, my hair had not naturally changed back to its normal color. Sometimes I thought I was getting used to it, and then my mother would look at it and sigh.

"I know," I said. "I keep thinking about using my designer jean money to get it dyed back to normal. I guess I'm out of time."

"I have another idea," Tara said. "Markers."

"No way," I said.

"Way."

"They'll just wash out," I said.

"Not if we use the permanent kind. There might be some in the art room."

I wasn't sure it was a good idea, but at least it was doing something with Tara. We walked down to the empty art room and finally found some black permanent markers on the teacher's desk. We went back to the bathroom.

"I'll just try a small part so if it looks weird, no one will notice," Tara said.

"It can't look any weirder than it already does, I guess."

Tara took a small clump of my hair and ran the marker back and forth over the orange part. She held it up in the mirror.

"It's working!" I said. I took another marker and started coloring the front while she worked on the back. The fumes started to give me a headache, but we kept coloring, even the underparts.

The funny thing about talking to someone working on your hair is that you're so close, but you don't make direct eye contact. Tara looked at me in the mirror.

"I still can't believe you messed with your hair," she said. "I've always wanted hair like yours."

"Mine?" I was pretty sure I had misheard.

"It's so pretty. No one in school has hair that looks like yours," said Tara. She picked up another strand of hair to color. "I'm jealous."

"Ha ha," I said. "I'm not the student superstar."

"But you've got this amazing voice. And the whole ensemble adores you because you're smart and funny, and you got them to sound twenty times better. And you started a business, which I would never have had the guts to do. I just tag along and hope you don't mind."

"I started the business so I could have designer jeans, like yours," I said.

Tara made a *pffft* noise. "Anybody can buy something."

"I always thought you were the Royal in the Royal We," I said.

"Nope," said Tara. "Both of us."

We were quiet again, but this time it was the good kind of quiet instead of the bad kind. Tara colored another strand of my hair, then pointed into the mirror at a bathroom stall. I turned around to read it forward.

Ricky A.
+
~~Amanda~~
~~Chrissy~~
Jennifer

"I guess Ricky was cast right, as Elvis the Heartthrob," I said. "But which Jennifer?" Every class I was in had at least one Jennifer, and so did our play.

"Red-haired Jennifer," said Tara. Red-haired Jennifer didn't seem like the type of person to write on a bathroom door. But I was pretty sure that Chrissy was Chrissy Wright. It was easy to picture her crossing out Amanda's name.

"What if," I said. Then I paused.

"What if what?"

"What if we changed the words to one of your songs so that someone else could sing it," I said. "Someone else, like me." This was huge, asking Tara to give up one of her songs.

She hesitated. "Which one?"

"'All-American Town.' We're already onstage."

"Mrs. Tyndall would probably kill us." Tara, the teacher's favorite.

"But only after we do it," I said. A bigger idea was beginning to take over. "And we should include some of the others in the ensemble."

Tara nodded. "Let's do it." She capped her marker and fluffed my hair. "What do you think?"

I had never liked straight black hair more.

"You are a True-Blue friend," I said, "for turning my hair black."

"You know," said Tara, "I kept telling myself that as long as we said things were okay that we'd be okay. That we'd stay True-Blue friends. But this is better." She didn't mean hair color.

"Maybe that's what True-Blue is," I said.

"Making mistakes?"

"Fixing them," I told her. "Fixing them together."

CHAPTER 34

OUR ALL-AMERICAN TOWN

CALL TIME FOR FRIDAY'S PERFOR-mance was at five, but Tara wasn't there.

I practiced all her solos in case she didn't make it from oratory in time. Mrs. Tyndall kept looking at her watch from a chair in the corner. She sat very straight.

Finally Tara ran in, wearing her pink oratory dress, while we were doing warm-ups.

"Well?" I said.

"Fourth." She didn't look as sad as I thought she would.

"Sorry," I said.

"There's always next year," she said. "We have other things to think about."

I grabbed her arm and pulled her into the circle.

"Welcome to our play," Tiffany said, onstage alone before the curtains opened. She was doing a number of Mrs. Tyndall's jobs because of the back situation. "We'd like to take you back to the 1950s, to a little all-American town called Pleasant Valley."

The audience broke into applause, the curtains opened, and we stepped into the blinding light. I tried to spot the people I knew were there: my parents and my grandmothers, hopefully without any animal accompaniment. David's friend Scott had come to see Hector and to not see David, who spent all his time backstage. Mrs. Mather, the T-shirt lady, was out there somewhere, along with Mr. Pickens, our neighbor. But with the lights onstage and the darkness beyond, it was hard to make anyone out. And then the audience kind of disappeared, and the only thing left was the music.

We launched into "Everything Is Still the Same" and hit every cue. Tara was amazing as Brenda Sue. And David and Mr. Shea had been right about embracing mediocrity—as long as they were smiling, Duncan, Max, and Andy looked like they were dropping their hoops on purpose.

"We're doing it, we're doing it," I said when we finished the first act.

The second act passed even faster. Tara nailed her solos. And she pronounced *Imogen* exactly right.

Finally we got to "All-American Town," when Brenda Sue was supposed to be center stage while we swayed in the background. But the Royal We had changed the setup, with Tiffany's help.

For a minute, I was filled with terror. First because Mrs. Tyndall might kill us for changing her words. And second, what if Mrs. Tyndall was right? Maybe I would confuse the audience. Maybe I didn't belong.

I felt a cool hand squeeze mine.

"Are we ready?" Tara said.

"We are," I said.

Tara took the red scarf out of her hair and wrapped it around my ponytail.

I put my Vincent Chin button on my sleeve, where I could see it and be brave.

The music started. Mrs. Tyndall wasn't moving her head very quickly, so it probably took her a minute to realize that Tara wasn't out front where she normally was; she was in the back with the rest of us.

I walked to the front and sang the first part:

My town's an all-American town,
We all say "how do you do?"
We welcome friends old and new.

I walked back to the group and Duncan took over:

My town's an all-American town,
Where I get to share my vision
Of Technicolor television.

Then Hallelujah came to the front. We didn't change the words for her part, but when she sang it, it had a different meaning. A better one.

> *My town's an all-American town,*
> *Where we're on the same team,*
> *And we all have a dream.*

Then we all came together for the end, with Hector and Tara and Jennifer and Kelli Ann, and Ricky swinging his hips in a leather jacket:

> *Our town's an All-American town,*
> *Where we find inspiration*
> *In a new innovation.*
> *What took us so long?*
> *How could we be so wrong?*
> *You can see our hips shakin',*
> *And there's just no mistakin',*
> *We're an all-American town!*

We were supposed to be singing about Hula-Hoops. But that night, in front of the crowd and Mrs. Tyndall, it felt like we were singing about ourselves as we held the Hula-Hoops high over our heads, showing the audience that not everyone looked exactly the same in Pleasant Valley, Tennessee. But we still all belonged there. Maybe some of us were not considered stars, but together we were a constellation.

We're an all-American towwwwwwn!

The audience burst into applause, rising from their seats. It was an excellency, a thousand times over.

When we ran offstage, Tara and I hugged.

"I can't believe we did it," I said.

"We did! We did!"

"Yes," Mrs. Tyndall said. "You did." It sounded like an accusation. She was on her feet once again, looming over us, looking fierce. She didn't yell at us for destroying her play. But she didn't say anything positive, either. She just stood there, staring, as the principal hurried up to her.

"Edna," he said. "What a triumph. A triumph. Kids, you were glorious. I expect a repeat performance tomorrow!"

Tara and I looked from the principal to Mrs. Tyndall, who was still staring at us like a cobra ready to strike. She twisted her lips together, hard. And then she nodded her head a single time and thumped her cane. It was her reluctant seal of approval. Our version of the play was getting an encore! Tara and I hugged again, and my hair caught on something. As I tried to untangle myself, I saw what it was. Tara was wearing a Vincent Chin button, too.

"Where'd you find that?" I asked.

"I found it on the floor," said Tara. "I figured you meant to give it to me but forgot."

I had made a button for Tara, but I had left it in my jewelry box when I thought she didn't care about Vincent.

But there it was. Maybe one of the boys had dropped theirs.

Or maybe.

Ghost.

CHAPTER 35

SUPPOSED-TO

AFTER OUR PERFORMANCES ON Saturday, we had a cast party, better known as popcorn and punch in the art room. I made buttons as presents for the cast and crew.

With some prodding from Tara, I even gave one to Mrs. Tyndall. She put on the button and then straightened her sweater.

"Thank you," she said politely.

"You're welcome," I said, just as politely.

"That was quite a change," she said, finally talking about it. "What you did with 'All-American Town.' You were lucky that the audience responded as positively as they did."

And Mr. Hoban, too, I thought.

I sighed. It was clear that Mrs. Tyndall hadn't gotten our point from the dancing. But she kept talking. "You might have a career as a choreographer."

I knew it was a compliment, but that wasn't what I had in mind.

"I think we'll do *Alice in Wonderland* next year," Mrs. Tyndall said. "More age appropriate, I think. And with an eighties update."

I imagined the Cheshire cat saying things like *tubular.* And I thought about my mom, who wanted to stand up for other people. And me. But I'd promised her I'd stand up for myself.

"Alice doesn't have to have blonde hair and blue eyes," I said.

Mrs. Tyndall's eyes—which were not blue themselves—widened. "That's the way Alice has always . . ."

"It's Wonderland," I said. "Let people wonder."

After the party, I walked to the car with my family. There was a spring chill, which made the stars look extra bright.

"This look was my favorite," David said, doing a very good impression of me looking adoringly at Elvis Presley.

"You're our superstar," Mom said, which is a thing moms are supposed to say.

"You know what will make you a star?" Safta said. "Work."

"And luck," said Wai Po. She pulled a newspaper from her purse and handed it to me.

For a second, I thought it would have something to do with Vincent Chin. But it was a current newspaper, and inside was a small notice that had been circled three times:

Star Search:
Open Auditions!

Do you have incredible talent?
Put it on display in front of real talent scouts.

Thursday, May 24, at 3 p.m.

Jefferson Civic Center

Actors! Dancers! Singers! Models! Comedians!

"That's in five days," I said.

Wai Po and Safta nodded.

"What would I wear?" But I knew the answer before the words finished going into the air. The Nudie suit.

"We stitched our names on the back pocket," said Safta.

"It's designer," Wai Po told me.

I pictured myself onstage in the shiny red suit. It was different but not necessarily bad. There was another, bigger issue.

"What would I sing?" I asked.

"What do you want to sing?" asked Dad.

"Patsy," I said. After all the sadness of not singing, and the joy of returning to song, I could finally sing Patsy the way I wanted to. I wouldn't sing it the way she did, but the way only I could.

I turned and walked backward in front of my parents. "So you'd be willing to let your one and only Chinese Jewish daughter put on a homemade Nudie suit and sing country music in front of a huge, possibly national, audience?"

"Isn't that how all great musicians get their start?" teased Mom.

"I might be the first one with this start. But I'm okay with that," I said.

"That's the secret," said Wai Po. "You are someone they've never seen before."

"There's only one Lauren Horowitz," Safta said.

"Lauren Le Yuan Horowitz," corrected Wai Po.

I looked at my parents and my grandmothers. In front of us, David was walking with his friends, trying to catch up to Kelli Ann without being obvious about it. Tara, my True-Blue best friend, was handing out buttons with her mom. "Buchanan for mayor!"

"Hey, Lauren," Duncan yelled. "Wait up."

All around us, people were shouting and laughing.

And that was a supposed-to I was okay with. Because in that moment, with my friends and family around me and all of the possibilities in front of me, everything felt like it was exactly the way it was supposed to be.

SHAKE IT UP

Abridged, Junior Version

Words and music by Edna Tyndall

Act I

Hoopla

Jumping through Hoops

All-American Town

Everything Is Still the Same

Intermission

Act II

Normal American Boy

The King Is Coming

In the Middle of the Circle

Circling through Time

All-American Town (reprise)

Director: Edna Tyndall

Stage Manager: Tiffany Ellison

Brenda Sue Parker: Tara Buchanan

Imogen: Jennifer Gallagher

Theodore Goreson: Hector Clelland

Elvis Presley: Ricky Almond

Mayor McArdle: Paul Giardino

Mr. Parker: Max Burka

Mrs. Parker: Amy Coleman

Greg Parker: Trey Coleman

Russian Ambassador: Andy Jenkins

Mrs. Goreson: Julie Sinclair

Elvis's Publicist: Kelli Ann Majors

Town Moms: Mia Andrews, Angela Nardonne, Liz Figley, Kelli Ann Majors

Ensemble: Cheryl Vickers, Lila Mahoney, Lauren Horowitz, Duncan Stowell, Andy Jenkins, Hallelujah Simmons, Michael Spiers

Lights: Henry Rowan, Chuck Saunders

Sound: Zahir Krauser

Prop Master: Tina La Piana

Curtains: Chloe Koenig

Hoop Wrangler: David Horowitz

Patrons:

To a Tee: We make 'em while you wait!

Holmes's Hardware: For All Your Needs, From Nails to Seeds!

Harrington Law Firm

Kay Buchanan for Mayor: Buchanan Cares!

Sandell Sporting Goods

WTRY: Where Country Is Cool

The Spaghetti Tree Restaurant

Love Notes:

Kudos, Tara! This is just the beginning!
   Mom, Dad, Grandma, and Jay

Edna, Brava, as always.
   Hugh

Felicidades, Hector!
   Love, Mamá, Papá, y Alonso

Hallelujah—We are so proud of you!
   Mom, Dad, and Dwayne

Cheryl, You sing like an angel. There's no height you can't reach!
    Mom

Now do you have time to do your homework, Duncan?
    Mom, Dad, Melissa, and Toby

The guy who works the spotlight shines the brightest!
    Mom and Robert

Michael, Well done!
    Gigi

The milk was not my fault!
^It was mine. Hahahaha.
Totally awesome, Tiff!
    Dad and Claire

Shake it, Ricky!
    Love, The Ricky Almond Fan Club

Chloe, The show could not go on without you opening that curtain!
    Love, Dad

Well done, Max!
    Mom, Dad, Ethan, and C. J.

Dear Lauren, You will always be our star! We love you.
    Mom, Dad, Safta, Wai Po, and the Hoop Wrangler

ACKNOWLEDGMENTS

To everyone who has been there for us all along, thank you. Our wonderful editor, Lisa Sandell, and the encouraging crew at Scholastic. Our agents, Susan Cohen and Tracey Adams, who are always warmly supportive. Our Wednesday morning critique group, where we have shared much more than stories. Our families: David, Matthew, Jason, and Kate Harrington, and Butch, Graham, and Karina Lazorchak; our moms and brothers and in-laws! Some of our writing friends went the extra mile for us this year. We love you. Sara Lewis Holmes: You need to start teaching. Thank you to Amy Yam, DVM, for sharing your knowledge of how things go. Special thanks to our beta readers: Elisa Rosman, Camille Saperstein, Lucia Saperstein, and Evelyn Khoo Schwartz. And to every teacher, librarian, or bookseller whose heart flutters every time they match a kid with the right book: Thank you from the bottom of our own fluttering hearts.

ABOUT THE AUTHORS

Madelyn Rosenberg is the author of *Dream Boy*, co-written with Mary Crockett, and many other books for younger readers, including the How to Behave books and *Cyclops of Central Park*. She writes books, articles, and essays for children and adults, and you can visit her online at madelynrosenberg.com.

Wendy Wan-Long Shang is the author of *The Great Wall of Lucy Wu*, which was awarded the Asian/Pacific American Librarians Association Award for Children's Literature, and *The Way Home Looks Now*, an Amelia Bloomer List selection and a *CCBC Choices* List selection. Visit her online at wendyshang.com.

Madelyn and Wendy cowrote the companion to this book, *This Is Just a Test*, which is a Sydney Taylor Honor Book. They both live in the suburbs of Washington, DC.

Lauren's brother, David, has a lot to deal with, between his dueling grandmothers, fighting friends, and confusing identities in *This Is Just a Test*, also by Wendy Wan-Long Shang and Madelyn Rosenberg!